COMING UP ROSES

by SARAH LAING

VINTAGE

Thank you to: my family, Jonathan, Otto, Gus, Robyn, William, Melissa, Tim, Elizabeth and Eve; the NZSA assessment programme; Helen, my original writing friend; my New York writing group, Marcia, Beryl and Nigel; my Wellington writing group, Alison, Caren, Johanna, Lynn and Raewyn; Griet and Louise; Harriet Allan and Rachel Scott.

A catalogue record for this book is available from the National Library of New Zealand

A VINTAGE BOOK
published by
Random House New Zealand
18 Poland Road, Glenfield, Auckland, New Zealand
www.randomhouse.co.nz

Random House International
Random House
20 Vauxhall Bridge Road
London, SW1V 2SA
United Kingdom

Random House Australia (Pty) Ltd
20 Alfred Street, Milsons Point, Sydney,
New South Wales 2061, Australia

Random House South Africa Pty Ltd
Isle of Houghton
Corner Boundary Road and Carse O'Gowrie
Houghton 2198, South Africa

Random House Publishers India Private Ltd
301 World Trade Tower, Hotel Intercontinental Grand Complex,
Barakhamba Lane, New Delhi 110 001, India

First published 2007

ISBN 978 1 86941 920 2

Design: Sarah Laing, www.poppyshock.com
Layout: Elin Bruhn Termannsen
Cover illustration and design: Sarah Laing
Printed in Australia by Griffin Press

To Jonathan

CONTENTS

you huff & rustle like a chips packet

AFTER BIRTH

It's Good Friday when you wrench your way into the world and lie on the delivery table, your eyes closed. Your head is a hairball dug out of a drain, your skin smudged with wax and blood. Everything is closed — all the shops and the museums, the sushi bars and veterinary clinics. Even the churches have bolted their doors, and I have a song in my head that won't go away, about dying on Good Friday, holding each other tight.

They lie you on my chest and you huff and rustle like a chip packet and still you won't open your eyes. I don't believe you have any. I want to peel back your lids with my thumb because I saw you on screen when you were telecast from space and there was nothing there, only dark hollows. Your head is scabbed from when they scraped your skin to test your pH level, and I think of the beer I baptised myself with to make my hair silky and balanced, a perfect 5.5.

The pediatrician says your lungs are like a bag that won't fully inflate and that's why you're making that funny noise. I remember the mince pies I had for school lunches, the loud bang the brown paper would make when popped. If you don't stop making that noise you will be taken away from me; you will be put in a plastic carton in the sandwich shop of half-made babies.

Your lungs have quieted so you are returned to suckle, and I ask your father *Does he have eyes? Yes,* he says. I don't believe him, and you won't drink so a woman is called to help. She has a cloche of white curls and glasses on a gold chain, and she describes my breasts as meat patties, and your lips the split bun. I squash the burger into your mouth. But still you won't drink so she harvests the colostrum with a syringe, droppers it into your mouth. She says that I am to take off all your clothes and lie you on my bare chest, to snuffle your way up to my breast when you are ready.

I try that when I am returned to the ward, pushed into my bed because my legs have been deadened. But the midnight midwife is angry at me for letting you get cold and she confiscates you, sealing you in the nursery sandwich carton. She is so angry at me that she lets me go to the bathroom by myself, and when I spill blood all over the white tiles I have to mop it up with towels thinned by bleach. I tell her I need you back to breastfeed, but she has already given you a bottle of formula. I try to express colostrum for later, and she pinches her lips and purses my nipples, telling me that I am doing it all wrong. She squeezes out a few drops and says there's nothing more there.

I have nothing, not even a baby. I lie in my green room with the clock that ticks loudly enough to remind you of my heartbeat. I look at the full moon through the curtain crack but there is no cow jumping over it, and I still haven't seen your eyes. I giggle at my wrists, which bleed from catheter wounds on Good Friday. I cry because there are no flowers for us and your father has gone home. I don't sleep until you are returned with a warning, *Don't you go taking off his clothes again; he doesn't have any fat on him to keep him warm.*

I have you all to myself now, forty hours after they first applied the gel to make you come early. You didn't want to come at all, and still you shiver and peep, scared of this air which is so easy to fall through, scratched by the cotton and wool, not fooled by the clock. I rise on my half-dead legs and look at you, wondering whether you really are mine. You open your eyes and look back.

a ballpoint pen digs
a blue hole into her
shoulder blade

THE WRONG SHOE

Ella flies into New York City on September 17, six days after the twin towers collapsed. It's a strange time to come. There are shrines everywhere, and stories that people intone like prayers. The blisters from the high-heeled walk over the Brooklyn Bridge, the smoke viewed from rooftops, the suburban storms of burnt paper, fragments of lost memoranda. *I saw the second plane hit*, they say. Candles from the Latin American specialty aisles in supermarkets flicker on the streets under heapings of roses, beside hand-crayoned notes.

I miss you, Jimmy, big brother. God Bless America. Fire engines drive as slowly as hearses; cars have flags tied to their aerials. Ella feels odd, then under suspicion, excluded by an event she only viewed on television.

She's always felt like that, even in the streets of Wellington. She saw the fires lit in other people's living rooms and she wanted to be eating chocolate biscuits in their armchairs. She saw girls in bars with black coils of hair and wanted to be them. She'd want to go home with their handsome boys, who would pull off the girls' painted-on dresses, the inkiness staining their pale carpets. Ella would turn back to her table of friends, her own boy that she may or may not take home, and feel so mismatched, her body a too-small shoe pinching her soul.

She's here now, in a place she had thought was vacuum-sealed in movie screens. It's a quieter, more fearful version of itself, but the people who have moved to Westchester to hide and have babies have made room for her. Soon she will be pinning Carrie Bradshaw roses to her lapel and writing witty columns for the *New Yorker*. Her ratty Brooklyn sublet is temporary. The bagel and cream cheese her diminishing funds afford her is slimming. She's sacrificed three lunches ($5.43) on peroxide. It will strip away her former self, making her blonde and new.

Ella rides the subway to Manhattan, her résumés for bartender/nanny/literary assistant/MTV host filed in her bag. An evangelist gets on at Dekalb Avenue. He has a strong West Indian accent, and chants, 'You gotta believe in Jeeee-sus, you gotta believe in Jeee-sus, you gotta let 'im into yo heart.' It sounds like a reggae song to Ella's ears. As the train bursts out of the tunnel and onto the bridge, the evangelist points at the places where the twin towers used to be. 'You tink da people knew dat day would be deir last? Da people in da plane? Da people in da street? Da people in da tower? You tink da people knew dat judgement day was 'ere? You gotta believe in Jeee-sus, let 'im into yo heart.'

Ella takes a little brochure from the man. It's a

cartoon, like her childhood Archie comics. The non-believers are poo-smeared, wafts of stink rising from their bodies. They become clean and sweet-smelling when they open the door to the Kingdom of God. Ella turns the brochure over, half-expecting sea monkeys and X-ray specs. There's a number for a church. She thinks of the girls from school who went to youth group to find boy-friends. They went to camps together and cried and fainted, spoke in tongues. They returned home exorcised and exfoliated. Ella always thought demon-casting was selfish. The devils would only find another adolescent girl to possess. It was like dropping your gum on the pavement.

Ella gets off at Union Square, and pushes through the people, past the stalls of chives and arugula, yellow cheddar and crusty bread. She stops to try some homemade jam on a cracker, and as she's sampling another flavour, trying to recast her hunger as curiosity, someone touches her shoulder.

'Heather, is that you?'

She turns and looks. A tall, delicate man with spiky black hair is staring at her.

'Remember? 1998. The train from Vienna to Barcelona? You sat next to me. We talked all the way?'

Ella has never been to Barcelona, but she has seen a movie about it and she owns a book on Gaudí. She smiles, wondering what kind of girl she is about to become. And how long it will take him to realise something's up.

'Barcelona was beautiful,' she says.

'What are you doing here?' the man asks. 'On vacation?'

'No, I live here.'

'I thought you lived in London.'

No one can pick her accent here. And she's heard her friends' London stories so often she feels like she can fake it. 'No, I moved. Just after September 11.'

'Oh. Terrible time to come. But New York's still a great city. Why move, though? I thought you loved London.'

'I do, I do, but sometimes you get sick of blowing your nose and seeing your snot come out black. Sometimes you can't take another vindaloo after a big night out on the turps.'

'It's the little things, huh? Oh my god, Heather, I can't believe it's you. Do you wanna go for a drink?'

Ella looks at her watch. It's two in the afternoon. The job hunt can wait another day. 'All right,' she says.

The man takes her to a bar on Fourteenth Street. It used to be a beauty parlour and the old-fashioned hair-dryers are still screwed to the wall. He asks her what she wants and she knows she should ask for a cosmopolitan. It comes with a maraschino cherry and an orange slice. He orders a beer.

'So what have you been doing since Barcelona?' Ella asks.

'I'm working on my product. I've got people in China manufacturing it as we speak. But it's pre-launch, so I gotta be careful about what I say.'

'Can't you give me a clue?'

'You're not going to find out any more than last time you asked me,' he replies. 'And then I told you too much. Anyone would think you were an international spy.'

'I'd be a lousy spy because I have a memory like a sieve. I can't even remember your name.'

He widens his eyes at her. 'It's Mario. I didn't think you'd forget. And I'm making a toy. I told you last time.'

'A toy? Like Barbie?'

'No, not like Barbie. More like PlayStation. We got a movie script in development to coincide with its launch. We're running that out of the LA studio. I go to Asia a lot to oversee production.'

'But you live here, right?'

'Yeah, I live in the East Village. Next to the best bagel shop in town. Wakes me up every morning. Smells good, though. You should go there.'

'Maybe I will,' says Ella.

Mario smiles. He drains beer, laughs at the cherry stone, the orange peel that Ella chews on. She's feeling a little dizzy. Where are the bar snacks? The cheese-flavoured fish, the peanuts?

'Another round?' he asks.

'Sure,' says Ella. 'I'll get it.'

'No, please, allow me.' Mario waves a $20 bill at the bartender. 'So where's your daughter?' he asks.

A daughter? This is getting tough. 'She's with her father, my ex. I miss her a lot.'

'But you told me her father was dead.'

'Did I? I probably meant I wished he was dead. The custody battle did my head in.'

'You were going to La Sagrada Familia. A private memorial. That's what you said. An architect, right? He'd fallen off scaffolding on the building he designed the year before. You said I reminded you of him and I cried, remember? You gave me your handkerchief. I still have it, see?' Mario fishes around in his pocket and withdraws a red tartan man's handkerchief, stiffened with snot. 'Here.

I meant to give it back, but I couldn't bring myself to.'

'Please, keep it,' says Ella. This poor, sensitive, beautiful man. She can't do this any longer. 'I'm not Heather, Mario. My name is Ella. And I've never been to Barcelona.'

Mario chokes on his beer. He puts it down, snorting. His face reddens. 'What the fuck? Are you trying to take me for something? Get out of here.'

'I just wanted to talk, that's all. Like you did to Heather,' says Ella.

'Jesus! What medication are you on?' He pushes back his barstool, grabbing his coat.

'Stop, Mario. I'm sorry, I thought this was an elaborate pick-up.'

'I was *empathising* with Heather, not hitting on her.'

'Were you? I've just got here. I don't know anybody. I thought you looked cute — you seemed like the kind of guy I would like to, you know . . . ' She puts her hand on his arm and flutters her eyelashes, gluggy with mascara.

Mario looks at her and shakes his head, turning to walk away. Then he stops. He lays his coat on the barstool next to him. He takes a sip of beer.

'Let me tell you about Heather,' Mario breathes into Ella's ear. 'She was a little uptight. You're not like that, are you?'

'No.' Ella gulps.

'So . . . shall we?'

She's not that kind of girl. But maybe the blonde Ella is. 'Let me powder my nose.'

In the bathroom Ella shakily applies lipstick and finger-combs her hair. Does she really want to sleep with this guy, or is she just relieved that he hasn't slapped her? And this is New York City — Mario probably has Aids. She checks which underwear she's wearing. Pink cotton. Why didn't she wear her black satin ones? With any luck they'll tear each other's clothes off, leaving a Hansel and Gretel trail across his apartment. Then they'll make crazy love, and before you know it, Ella will have a boyfriend, a free bagel breakfast and a life to slip into like a new pair of shoes. Manolo Blahniks maybe, or Jimmy Choos. Something she'll have to take a taxi in.

She emerges from the bathroom, observing how Mario's spine curves out of the red barstool, how he picks at the beer bottle label. He must be nervous too.

'Here we are,' says Mario, fumbling with keys, pushing her through the doorway. He kisses her in his kitchenette, her job-hunting dress pressed up against the sticky, crumbed bench, covered in takeaway boxes. As Mario's lips explore her neck she examines his apartment. There are comic books on the wall, hung by silver bulldog clips. There are racks of comic books next to the sofa. There are beer crates of comic books in precarious towers. In the corner of the room a cardboard cutout of Wookie from *Star Wars* stands guard.

Mario's lips are a lot harder than they look. His chin prickles her breast. She sticks her hand down the back of his trousers. His bum is soft and warm but he clenches it at her touch.

It's strange to be seduced in the afternoon light. Ella's eczema blares in her elbows. Mario pulls her onto the sofa, where a ballpoint pen digs a blue hole into her shoulder blade. He marks out the circles formed by her nipples and belly button, explores the trigonometry of her hipbones and pubis.

'You have a condom, don't you?' she asks him, but he doesn't answer. 'You have to wear a condom, please.'

'Heather,' he breathes, as his penis bumps and nubs its way inside her.

Ella wakes up to the sound of the keys in the door. She hadn't realised that Mario had left. She is covered by a cotton sheet. She half sits up, unsticking a comic book from her cheek. Mario is standing over her, a paper bag in hand.

'What time is it?' Ella asks.

'Seven-thirty. Here, have this.' He hands her a warm bagel wrapped in greaseproof paper.

'Shit! Seven-thirty in the morning?'

'No, seven-thirty at night.'

Ella unwraps it, butter dripping between her fingers. Mario eats one filled with cream cheese. 'Do you want to swap halves? I didn't know which you'd prefer.'

'This is fine,' says Ella, rivulets running down her chin.

'Listen, I gotta go to work, so you should leave too.'

'Work? But it's seven-thirty!'

'It's the time difference thing. I gotta be talking to the manufacturers in China during their working hours.'

'Can you speak Cantonese?'

'No, nor Mandarin. But the floor manager speaks English.'

'Are you sure you can't give me any more clues about what you're making? I'm probably going to be working as a waitress; it's unlikely I'd be able to sell your trade secrets.'

'Look, Heather, my parents don't know any more than

you do.'

'It's Ella.'

'Ella. Anyway, I'm going now, but if you like you can take a shower before you leave. Just close the door behind you; it locks automatically.' Mario leans towards her and kisses her buttery lips. 'Mmmm,' he says. At the door he turns. 'Leave your number,' he says. 'I'll call you.'

Ella walks down Second Avenue, her hair wet from the shower. She thinks of the note she left, depicting herself as a kind of *Powerpuff Girl*, but with breasts. She hopes he calls. Then again, Heather never put out, and he still carries around her handkerchief.

The night is crisp, and Ella is not scared of muggers. She walks past restaurants filled with beautiful people laughing and eating. Right now, she doesn't want to be at their tables, inside their skin. She's quite happy with her own, and that swollen ache between her legs. Her hair feels radiant, moon-coloured. Her dress clings to her curves, as do appreciative gazes. She feels hungry and lucky, like she's going to find a job tomorrow. She wants to captivate others from a café window. She'll go to the Moroccan place with the *Village Voice* recommendation down St Mark's Place.

'How many?' the maître d' asks.

'One,' Ella replies. He tries to send her to the back of the restaurant, to where the doors swing into the kitchen. 'No,' she says, 'I want to sit there.' The maître d' grudgingly complies, tossing the menu at her as she sits down.

'May I tell you about the specials tonight, madam?' asks a different waiter. Ella's eyes are closed; she inhales the rich spice. 'We have a bastilla, a delicacy of ouarka pastry and pigeon meat, dusted in sugar . . .'

The words roll over Ella's tongue, saliva springing to greet prunes, almonds and fennel bulbs. This might be better than eating. When she hears what she most wants, she opens her eyes.

'Mario?' she says.

'Hassan,' he replies.

'No, no, you're Mario.'

'Would you like to order now? Or do you need some time?' His face remains impassive, defying recognition. Why won't he acknowledge her? It was only a few hours ago that she tucked that lock of hair behind his ear.

'I'm Ella, don't you see? We had sex. I'm sorry about Heather, but if this is your idea of a joke . . . you know me!'

Ella hears her voice as though it's in another room, ringing through the walls. Other diners turn to look.

'Madam, please, I must ask you to calm down. You have me mistaken. Now, would you like an appetiser to start?'

'Actually, I've changed my mind.' Ella pushes back her chair and gathers her bag in a clumsy embrace, knocking another customer's wine across his plate of couscous. She runs out of the restaurant. The door tinkles as Mario runs after her.

'Madam, madam?' he calls.

She stops and turns.

'You forgot your coat.'

She doesn't move. She watches him as his extended arm drops. He shrugs, turns, then something catches his eye. He lays the threadbare coat over a homeless man in an alcove, his head rising and falling on the belly of an Alsatian.

Lauren finds herself in the unlikely position of doing Vasilisa's makeup.

BIRD SONG

STARLING

'What do you think of Vasilisa?' Barbara asks Lauren, the night Lauren touches the tumour in Barbara's groin.

'She seems young.' Lauren thought she wasn't much older than a child. Her bones were green branches to be pushed past on a path. She had penciled leaf shapes around her eyes. She was dressed in a short skirt, even though it was cold outside. Maybe it seemed warm to her compared with Russia, but her legs were mottled, and she had goosebumps where hairs once grew.

'She's twenty, you know.'

'That's a big gap.'

Patrick is forty-five. Lauren and Jack had decided he must be gay.

'He seems quite taken with her. Strokes her as if she's a cat. She might bite him if he doesn't watch out. Oh.' Barbara winces. 'I think I should go to bed.'

Lauren heaves Barbara out of the armchair, her slight build a 45-degree counterpoint to Barbara's bulk. She had thought cancer would waste Barbara away. But Barbara's fat has been replaced by fluid, pooling in her ankles and wrists, bloating her tummy. Her breath is difficult in Lauren's ear and, because the builder cut costs twenty years ago, skimping on hall widths and bedroom sizes, they cannot walk side by side to Barbara's bedroom. Lauren must lead.

'It's pretty bad,' Barbara admits, after Lauren has helped her remove her dressing gown and turned down her thin polyester sheets. Lauren is surprised; Barbara is usually stoic, even masochistic in her acceptance of pain. 'It's got bigger, too.' She grabs Lauren's hand and guides her finger from one end of the tumour to the other. It is the shape and length of a banana.

'Oh my god,' Lauren says inappropriately. Barbara *believes*, and as a boy Jack was hit with the jug cord for saying *Jesus Christ*. There are devotional messages cross-stitched along the hall, and on the fridge there is a photocopied article by Reverend Brittle, damning to hell the drinkers, the gamblers, the homosexuals and the aborters. Lauren's had an abortion. 'Maybe you should go see the doctor again.'

'Yes, maybe I should.' She slips out her teeth and her mouth becomes a bullet-hole.

Lauren is too embarrassed to stay any longer. 'Goodnight,' she says, switching off the light.

MOREPORK

I watch myself through my bedroom window. Before I left, I switched the light on because I thought I would read. I toss one way, I turn the other. My sheet swaddles me.

Morepork.

My cry ricochets around the valley, and my son comes out onto the deck, searching for me on the branches of the pine, the flame tree, the pohutukawa.

Morepork.

The sky is clear, stars salting its blue-black belly. Through the kitchen window I see my daughter-in-law making a cup of tea. She grimaces at my cups; she's got airs and graces, frittering her money on fancy things. But she makes Jack happy, and they have a beautiful child. Polly is learning the violin and going to ballet lessons, something I longed to do. I am sorry I will not be here to visit as she grows.

Flying is like diving. I used to dive for scallops as a girl. They were very deep, but I could hold my breath for a long time, kicking my powerful legs to the sea floor. I would gather them up in a basket, then surface. I would eat some raw and take the rest back to the house, where my mother would fry them in butter for my father and younger siblings.

Morepork.

Jack has found me. He pulls Lauren outside too fast; her tea spills. She goes back inside to sponge her skirt and he is torn, the electric light spoiling his night vision.

CARRIER PIGEON

Lauren opens the wedding invitation a month later. Their names are scrawled in gold on cheap purple paper. The handwriting is foreign, echoing a Cyrillic script. Patrick wants to answer his mother's question before she dies. Yes, he will marry — a girl he has just met, who may or may not be after his passport.

Jack phones Patrick to RSVP. He paces the hall, kicking up Lauren's nerves. Lauren still doesn't know where Patrick found her. On the internet? At some club? Jack won't ask, and he won't stay in the same room as her because she will shout questions over him. Jack and Patrick are brothers but they only communicate via their mother. Lauren wonders how they will talk once she's gone.

Jack returns to the kitchen. Polly stares up at him as he maps out Barbara's new tumour, its cul-de-sacs and terraces. Although the wedding is not until the weekend, Jack wants to fly up the next morning. Lauren can't; she has an order of bed linen to dispatch, and new clients coming around to view Polly's showcase room. She will drive up on Friday.

WILD GOOSE

Polly is singing the same song over and over again in the back seat. Lauren puts on a CD to drown her out. The traffic slows and then stops, the state highway doubling as a small-town main street. An Armourguard truck reverses towards Lauren, but she can't find her horn. She waves and yells as the truck scratches the mint green paint off Jack's beloved Citroën. Polly looks stricken, and Lauren considers turning back at the thought of Jack's face. She doesn't want to go to the wedding anyway.

The driver who climbs out is sexy, yanking at his black rock-star fringe. He scream-swears, *Fucking-Jesus, cunt, mother fucker*. He kicks his tyre. Then, aggression spent, he approaches Lauren and smiles. 'I'm so sorry,' he says. 'It was totally my fault. Can I take down your details?'

A white-haired woman approaches him. 'Excuse me, young man, did I do something wrong?'

'No, ma'am, I was just venting my frustration at backing into this lady's car.'

'My husband's pride and joy. I'm in deep shit.'

'Oh, I am glad,' says the woman. 'I thought you were swearing at me.' She smiles at him, and climbs back into her red Honda.

By the time they reach the house, having missed their turn-off in the rain and driven an hour too far north, it is dark. Lauren carries a sleeping Polly to Jack's childhood bed. Lauren wants to be defused, but she sees that Jack needs comfort more, his shoulders slipping off their bone hanger. He kisses her urgently but she breaks away, wanting to see Barbara before she loses her nerve. She is relieved to find her asleep, not so changed in the dark.

Lauren sits down to a plate of nacho chips soggied by mince and beans. At home, the cooking is her responsibility. She wonders whether she should have encouraged Jack a little more.

Morepork.

'Can you hear that? I think it lives in a tree near here.'

'Mmm,' says Lauren, through a mouthful of grated

cheese. She watches Jack open the ranchslider and lean into the night sky.

TERN

Polly and Lauren escape the house early the next morning, taking Hector on his chewed leash. Hector is strong: part Alsatian, part Ridgeback. Couch-ridden for Barbara's decline, he yanks them down the hill and along the road. Moss tassels overhanging branches, tickling Lauren's face.

The mist vignettes the sea. On the wharf there is a cluster of elegant terns, intent on a mussel. Hector breaks away from Lauren's hand, snapping at a tern. Lauren and Polly yell at him to let go. Too late. The tern staggers to the end of the wharf, blood vivid against its white wing. It falls into the water. It drifts into the fog, the other terns orbiting their wounded mate.

'Can we save it, Mum? Should we dive in and grab it?' Polly asks. In the city they have nursed blackbirds to health. They have put sparrows with broken wings into shoeboxes.

PEACOCK

Lauren finds herself in the unlikely position of doing Vasilisa's makeup. The bride appeared on the doorstep at two, a couple of hours before the wedding. She was wearing jeans, her dress hanging over her thin forearm.

'You can help me?'

Lauren looks for Patrick, but he is at his house down the road. Funny he should finally find his own place when his mother really needs him. Jack had come home at 3am; they had decided upon a stag night after all. She had pulled him in off the deck — where he was singing to the moreporks — at four. His skin was ice.

'Sure I can,' says Lauren. 'But don't you have a bridesmaid?'

'No. It is not Russian tradition. But you will be my sister soon.'

'Well, maybe you should put on your dress so I can see what to do with your hair.'

'I know what to do with my hair. Come to the other room.'

Lauren looks for Barbara, who likes to grant permission. But she is drowsing fitfully in the other room, a methadone tablet stuck in her throat. Vasilisa takes Lauren's wrist and pulls her, and Lauren notices that her fingertips are clubbed, like frogs' feet. She pulls off her T-shirt and jeans. She is wearing underwear with a profusion of lace and flowers, clasps to be undone, straps that cut into her skin. She puts on her satin dress and turns around so Lauren can zip her up. The zip catches on threads.

'You made this dress?'

'Yes. Barbara, she give me her machine.'

'She did?' Lauren had been going to ask for it; she had already cleared a space in her basement studio. Not that it is a particularly good machine, but it would have been useful for when Lauren needs to hire temporary assistance to finish the next season's range. She wonders whether Barbara will be donating her wedding ring as well. She turns her own Mexican silver band in the groove it has ground for itself.

The sleeves are puffed, and a few of the pearls Vasilisa has stitched to the bodice fall off. Lauren picks them out of the carpet, along with grit and hair. The home help has not vacuumed this room. She is too busy sponge-bathing Barbara, rolling her from one side of her bed to the other to change the sheets. Lauren is glad it is not her.

'This must have taken you a while,' she says.

Vasilisa shrugs. 'You think is tight enough?'

The seams are straining. 'Yes,' says Lauren. Her own wedding dress was a loose 1920s shift in a soft green, and they had the reception at the art gallery.

Vasilisa presents Lauren with her makeup bag, and Lauren is confused by the palate of emerald and lavender and scarlet. She applies light bridal sheens to Vasilisa's lids, but Vasilisa scowls at the effect and asks her to put on more.

'Why don't you do it yourself?'

'I cannot,' Vasilisa says, demonstrating how her arms will not move in front of her.

'Do you love Patrick?' Lauren asks, painting a Hockney swimming pool over Vasilisa's left eye.

'He is good man. Yes, I will love him.'

'You *will* love him? You mean you don't already?'

'We only just met. But it is not so good to love hard when you marry. My parents, their love was fierce and then it turn inside out and they hate each other. The neighbours, they always complain. My mother throw the television out the window. It is better this way.'

'Where did you meet?' Lauren suspects the Russian brides website she found on a Google search. She is waiting for Vasilisa to confirm.

'At the Ceroc class. Is cheaper than language school,

good for chat. He was the only man; the other girls fight over him.'

'Patrick? Dance?' Lauren can't see it: his round belly doesn't suggest grace.

'He stand on my toe at first, but I think he improve. You will see. I teach him a Cossack dance for the wedding.' Vasilisa looks in the mirror. 'Yes, that is good. Thank you.'

'Shit!' Lauren remembers that she is meant to help Barbara get dressed; she is meant to do her makeup too. She doesn't want to — maybe that's why she blocked it from her mind. 'Here,' she says, putting the lipstick in Vasilisa's hand. She goes next door to wake Barbara.

Polly is sitting on the end of Barbara's bed. Barbara is awake, her pupils occupying too much of her irises. Polly is reading her *The Velveteen Rabbit*. It is Polly's favourite book. Her finger holds the words in place long enough to say them. She casts sidelong glances at a grandmother who always corrects her. But Barbara just lies there.

'Shall we get dressed, Barbara?'

Barbara's pupils roll like ball-bearings. '*No*', she groans.

'Come on, you have to. Patrick wants you to be at the wedding.'

Barbara barely shrugs. If. You. Must.

KINGFISHER

Now that my daughter-in-law has put my teeth in, my beak is long and sharp. She pushes my arm into a shiny blue sleeve and they are wings. I am on the power lines, my reclaimed breast a creamy yellow.

I look at the ciphers in the sea. I dive, and the sprat is mine, a silver sliver slithering down my throat. Sprats once wriggled on the ribs of the *Thomasina*. I didn't much like to sail; it turned my stomach. Harry did. He threaded silver on his hooks, exchanging sprats for marlin, tuna, hapuka and kahawai. He presented me their hefty bodies, bellies slit, scales still clinging. I filleted them. Too much fish. I froze it, I gave it to the neighbours. Harry packed the tin drum with manuka and smoked everything — my washing, my furniture, my hair.

Had I known that Harry would be dead when I got back from the dairy, I wouldn't have gone. I could have made up powdered milk. I could have forgone the daily paper. I would have said something. But what? What do you say? I am giving them plenty of warning, and still they don't know. They hold my hand even though I was never one for affection. They blather on, but I am sliding across currents that criss-cross my valley.

He was dead in his chair. I thought he had wet himself, but it was the tea I had made him before I left, black — three sugars. It spilt when his heart stopped.

CUCKOO

Lauren can't find Barbara's prosthetic breast. It is not under the bed, nor is it in the washing basket. She suggests that they stuff a sock down Barbara's bra, like she did as an eleven-year-old, trying to see her future. Barbara shakes her head, and Lauren is embarrassed by her suggestion. The makeup doesn't help. Beneath the powder she looks grey.

'How do you feel?' she asks.

'I don't know,' says Barbara. She can't say whether she is comfortable or uncomfortable. She doesn't know if she wants her feet up or down. She doesn't know whether she needs a pillow behind her head. Lauren must decide.

'Come into the living room. They're waiting for us.' They are going to do the photos before the ceremony, just in case. Patrick is clomping around, having shown Jack his boot full of vodka. 'Bride insisted,' he explained. Lauren wonders what Patrick's teetotalling aunties and uncles will make of it.

Lauren heaves Barbara up onto her walker and pushes her out the door.

Step.

Step.

Step.

It takes longer than Lauren can stand. She will ring the hospice tomorrow, ask them to deliver a hospital bed. The ancestors beckon from dark photographs that tile the hall. They have saved a seat for Barbara in the shadows. She can sit down if she likes.

'You're doing well. Keep on going,' says Lauren, as if talking to Polly. They break into the light of the living room. A few more steps and Barbara can slump into her chair.

Vasilisa is outside, imprinting her cigarette with scarlet. She sees Barbara and stamps it out beneath her gold stilettos. She expels the last breath of smoke and goes inside, taking Barbara's hand. 'Hello Mama,' she says.

Mama? But Vasilisa barely knows her; even Lauren calls her Barbara.

'It must be so hard for you,' says Barbara. That is the

most she has said all day.

'Yes,' says Vasilisa, the aquamarine of her eyes suddenly intensified. She squeezes Barbara's fingers.

Jack has two different cameras, his Pentax SLR and his Nikon digital. He fancies himself as a photographer — always photographs Lauren's range. After each crushing performance appraisal he talks about chucking in his government job, becoming a freelancer. But Lauren prefers at least one regular income.

'Okay, Paddy, get in behind Barbara. Next to your bride. Now where the hell did you get that shocker of a shirt?'

It is red satin with mother-of-pearl buttons. 'You like?' Patrick says.

'Sure thing, Santa. Hold on to your woman. Closer. That's it.'

Vasilisa is the leaf curling around the fat tulip bloom of Patrick. Their bridal attire clashes with the homely armchair, covered in a crocheted blanket. Below them, Barbara tries to smile but grimaces instead.

'Lovely, lovely,' says Jack. 'Polly, get into the picture. And you too, Lauren.'

Lauren has never felt part of this family but she stands among them anyway. They fan out behind Barbara. It doesn't seem like wedding photos. Lauren is reminded of the portraits the Victorians took of their dead.

'Take one of me and Mum,' says Jack, pressing the camera into Lauren's hand. 'Just push the button.'

Lauren fumbles; she's scared of Jack's machines. She will blur it or accidentally delete something and he will be angry, like he was when he saw the car. It doesn't take much these days. Jack will have his eyes closed; he looks drunk in photos.

But, scrolling through her shots, she sees Jack's eyes flash back at her. His mother's too, reflecting red light in her satellite-dish lenses. The smile has been dispensed with. There is a defiance, a reminder that when Barbara was well, she avoided the camera. 'No, I'm too fat and old and ugly,' she said. 'Don't photograph me.'

'Mama, you look beautiful,' says Vasilisa, and the smile bobs on the surface of Barbara's face, then sinks deep inside her.

'Mum, can I be a bridesmaid?' Polly asks.

Polly looks pretty in her sprigged white and red dress with its red sash to match her sandals. Lauren vetoed the cropped lilac top and frilled skirt that Polly requested.

'I don't think Vasilisa wants a bridesmaid.'

'Yes she does. I asked her. And look, I've found some flowers.'

Polly runs to the kitchen and comes back with a handful of swan plants, their green lanterns swinging off their stalks. She has wrapped their bottoms in silver foil.

'Yes, that is true,' says Vasilisa. 'I would like Polly to walk up the aisle with me. Otherwise I am lonely.'

'But the flowers . . . ' says Lauren.

'I did not think to get flowers,' says Vasilisa.

'Here, have some of mine,' says Polly, dividing her bunch in two.

'Thank you, darling.' Vasilisa kisses Polly in the crest of her hair. Polly beams up at her, and for the second time Lauren feels jealous.

PUKEKO

I will not go to the wedding. I will sit on my egg in the marsh. I will wait for the afterlife to hatch; I am tired of this one.

People call me a clumsy bird, always veering into cars, but I did not ask them to build their roads along my reedy home. I am a clumsy woman. My bones are heavy and flightless.

I compensated for my shortcomings. I prayed every night. I bottled the peaches that hung over the rivers. I sent my sons out in the punt and they returned with mounds of gold. I sliced until my skin flapped. I peeled until my palms were stained yellow. The air was thick and sweet and the jars tinkled among water bubbles.

People talked about Harry and me, I know they did. He was a handsome man. They thought he was too good for me. They thought he should have a heron for a wife, a waif on stick legs. A lady who minded her Ps and Qs and knew how to play tennis. They didn't see the cream I scooped off the milking bucket and onto his porridge. They remembered that I was a sharemilker's daughter, not the landed gentry. But we were once, until my father's farm was taken by the Depression.

I'm not saying things were perfect between Harry and me. Maybe Patrick was reluctant to marry because of all the yelling we did. But he's found someone now. She's a good girl and I'm sorry I cannot attend. I have my egg to keep warm.

BIRD SONG

PIWAKAWAKA

Lauren walks to the wedding alone. The road is matted with pine needles like fur on a dog's back. Polly has gone in the cream and maroon Chrysler with Vasilisa, and Jack is pacing the front of the church with Patrick.

Barbara has returned to bed. The home help, who lives down the hill, came at short notice. She is grateful for the money, even though it is so little. Nobody Lauren knows works for $8 an hour. The home help has five children and packs scallops three days a week in twelve-hour shifts. But she is happy to peel off Barbara's Mother of the Groom clothes; she is happy to flannel clean her face and pull the pilled sheets up underneath Barbara's armpits.

It is a beautiful afternoon. Green hills melt into the sea. Mangroves point their fingers to the blue sky. A fantail pirouettes, mouth open to catch bugs. Cars slow down to offer Lauren a lift but she shakes her head. She prefers to walk.

The church is colonial, tongues poked into grooves, a hundred years after they were cut. It is filled with Barbara's sisters and brothers, nieces and nephews, great-nieces, great-nephews. Only Barbara has made do with one grandchild.

Lauren sits in the back with what must be Vasilisa's friends. A Japanese girl in a ruffled skirt pulls off a long purple thumbnail and drops it into her handbag. Lauren flinches, even though she can see it is fake. Along from her sits a tall skinny boy wearing a Dead Kennedys T-shirt. She is pleased that someone will appreciate the vodka.

The pastor has a frizzy grey afro and is wearing a belted pastel-blue polyester suit. Lauren almost expects him to break out into a Motown number. He asks the congregation to stand, in Maori and English.

Vasilisa is silhouetted in the doorway, Polly prisming light behind her. The congregation turns as they walk up the aisle. Vasilisa clutches a bouquet of red roses that she must have bought from the bucket outside the dairy. Polly still has her swan plant lanterns. Patrick is glowing between Jack and the pastor, and although he beams at Vasilisa, there is an undercoat of anxiety. Why isn't his mother here? Why couldn't she have held it together one last time?

The wedding doesn't hold Lauren's attention. She picks up a cushion appliquéd with a biblical scene. She wonders who made it. Maybe she could commission a secular version for her next range. She turns it over and sees the initials 'B.S.' Barbara's crafts look kitsch in her house, but in this context they are beautiful. Barbara has crocheted a rug from blues and golds but Lauren will not inherit it. 'This is what I want to be buried in,' she has said.

The congregation holds its breath as Jack searches for the rings. He pats his chest, his legs; he lifts up a shoe. They grow agitated, thinking of the torn linings of their own pockets, and the holes in the floor of the church. How many marriages have rolled beneath these boards? Jack punches Patrick's arm. He waves the rings above his head like a World Cup trophy. The pastor smiles, even though this gag has run past him a hundred times before.

Out of the corner of her eye Lauren sees a flutter. A fantail.

Peep. It bangs against the glass. Don't come inside, she wills. Do not deliver your message. She resists the urge to jump up and pull the windows shut with their long ropes. As it is, the church is sticky. She is frozen with panic, even though she has confided in her friends that it would be better if Barbara died. Not today, though. Not now.

Peep. Peep.

Lauren forces her attention to the front of the church. Patrick has tried to put the ring on Vasilisa's left hand, but she offers her right one instead. Behind her, Polly scratches. Bugs have crawled out of her bouquet and are conducting their own wedding march up her arms.

SWAN

'*Gor'ko! Gor'ko!*' yells Lauren, drowning out the relatives, who toast with sparkling grape juice instead of champagne. Vasilisa explained that it was Russian for 'bitter', and that Patrick must sweeten the vine with a kiss. He bends her over his forearm in a move he learnt at Ceroc. '*Gor'ko! Gor'ko!*', the relatives say, sounding not in the least bit Russian. They sit on wooden chairs along paper-covered trestle tables, glancing longingly at the buffet.

Later the relatives get drunk: Vasilisa soused the trifle in brandy. She pays special attention to Lauren's glass, and flings her arm around her shoulder as if they have been friends for years. 'I will teach you to dance Russian style,' she promises.

It is exhilarating to jump. Polly bounces until her skirt parachutes, then falls into a teetotalling uncle carrying his third helping of pudding. She scoops the sponge-cream mess off her dress with her forefinger and eats it. Vasilisa drags relatives from their chairs, and they test out their tiptoes before scuttling back to their seats. Knees and ankles are offered as excuses. The wedding party thins as relatives retreat to their motels.

Vasilisa snorts and leaps up and down. 'You must not remember tonight,' she says, handing Lauren a bottle of vodka. 'That is a sign of good wedding.'

Lauren sneaks off to the toilet, abandoning the bottle. When she tries to unlock the cubicle she finds she cannot. 'Help, help! I'm stuck in here!' She thumps, she kicks, she makes a splintery sound but cannot break down the door.

'Pull the lock towards you, then jiggle,' she hears someone say. 'It's a bugger that way.'

Lauren wipes her hands on her dress and tries again. It slips open. She feels foolish. On the other side, a woman in a white apron smiles. 'Been caught like that myself. Felt like being buried alive.'

'Mmm,' agrees Lauren, running the tap over her shaking hands.

'Are you part of the groom's whanau?' she asks.

'I'm Patrick's sister-in-law,' says Lauren, words sliding together.

'There's a phone call. You can take it in the kitchen.'

'Did youse have a good time?' asks the home help when Lauren, Jack and Polly arrive home. Lauren cannot remember.

The doctor is on his way; the home help makes cups of tea. Jack phones people at their motels, but tells them not to come until morning. Polly folds and unfolds her legs on Barbara's chair. She chews a corner of her crocheted blanket, her dark eyes reflecting unwatched music videos. Grief sits uncomfortably on her: she is old enough to feel its weight.

Jack drinks his tea on the deck. He is listening.

Morepork.

Lauren cradles her cup on the edge of Barbara's bed. She looks the same. How could the home help tell she had gone? She touches Barbara's hand, and although it is cold, it is no colder than it was before.

Morepork.

Morepork.

Lauren is waiting for Jack to come and get her, to yank her onto the deck, to point at a fork in the flame tree, the hole in the pohutukawa.

But he doesn't come.

It was her favourite condiment,
she drizzled it on everything.

Freezer BURN

The summer I worked in the pie factory, I would return home with the soles of my shoes caked in mince. It would clog in the tread like dog poo. When I took the shoes off at the door, the cat would lick them. By the time I put them on again the next morning they would be clean.

It was my first job. My boyfriend had just left me. After a year living together in a tumbling-down flat where the walls were so thin we could hear the neighbour farting, he had taken the proceeds of his computer tutoring job and gone to South America to find a Spanish-speaking girlfriend.

I was abandoned to the sausage roll wrapping line. The tubes of uncut sausage rolls would arrive in plastic crate towers, dusted in flour, pale and squishy as an inner thigh. I would pick up one, wrap it in clingfilm, then place another beside it. Then another, and another, until six rolls formed a cylinder. The film was cut on a hot wire.

Mine would wrinkle and the sausage rolls would shift and sag; I would quickly transfer them to the waiting plastic crate before my fellow wrappers noticed. There were three to my right: Bo, a Thai woman pregnant for the second time to a soldier; grandmotherly Denise, whose husband Errol rocked his arthritic body on the La-Z-Boy while she worked; and a frizz-haired bogan called Lisa, who played Judas Priest on her car tapedeck. To my left was Simone.

Simone had wafted through my school two years ahead of me, with a distracted grace. I had wondered where she had gone. Her white face flickered on top of her candle-boned body. Her shoulders slumped to height-adjust herself; her consorts were shorter and plainer than she. Her voice was soft and I had to lean in to hear her. She told me how she had bought her boyfriend a mountain bike for Christmas, and she was looking forward to Boxing Day, when they could go biking through the hills to the place where you could catch eels. She was also giving him a CD, a new pair of jeans and a book; I was amazed at her generosity, given our lowly pay.

The factory manager surveyed us from his glass box like the captain of a pirate ship. The factory was owned by closed Brethren, but he was a cultist, making cigarette and custard square offerings to the small shrine in his office. He had given me the job within minutes of meeting me. I answered his questions confidently (no, no criminal convictions; yes, I can arrive on time); I filled his student labour quota; and I was happy to accept $7.98 an hour. He showed me how to punch in, my card a testimony to my interview lies (I was always five minutes late). He handed me two white aprons, one to wear and one to wash, and a couple of shower caps, like the ones my grandmother wore in the days between her hairsets. His cousin was the foreman, and he paced the floor ensuring that none of us dilly-dally-chitter-chattered too much.

I liked the cousin. His name was Dougal. He had completed two years of a religious studies degree before throwing it in. He had a certain softness about him, or maybe his university education made him more familiar to me. Why had he given it up? How could he enjoy this job? It seemed that he did. It took me a week to figure out that he was going to get Simone's Christmas presents.

My new role made me feel noble. While my friends were lounging on busted verandas, smoking pot and talking about the working-class struggle, I was amongst it. The only problem was getting through the eight-hour days, and then the overtime. I was so bored.

Or was I? The radio played the same songs over and over again, until the baker boys howled like wolves whenever Whitney Houston declared her eternal love. But the casual revelations were interesting.

'See this scar on my arm?' Bo said. 'I was holding a piece of sugar cane and this monkey, he try to grab it. But he got my arm instead. I scream, *aeeeiiii!* And he run away, a piece of my arm in his mouth.' She showed us the scar, and it was a ropey, curdled thing, the pink shocking against her smooth brown skin.

In the lunchroom the Brethrens sat at their own table, free of the newspapers that sullied others. I sat with Simone, who squirted Worcestershire sauce under the membrane of her mince pie. It was her favourite condiment; she drizzled it on everything, and had suggested to management that they add it to the meat mix.

Bo struggled to squeeze her ever-increasing bump behind our table, and offered us her rice, her chicken, her egg, her chilli. I accepted an egg, but never grabbed the pie I longed for off the conveyor belt. I was now a vegetarian. I remembered how much I loved to scoop up the mince with my potato chips at primary school. They were delicious because I was only allowed one bought lunch each term.

Lisa raced in with tallies of the number of orgasms she had achieved the previous night, and the origins of her mangled earlobe. Then she tore off: she had shoes to buy and a mother to visit, elaborate tasks to be pressed into the half-hour sandwich.

Denise ate her selection of savouries and muffins, and talked about what Errol watched on TV, and what he might like for dinner. I would see some of the girls from the pie packing machine, but most of them smoked in the basement below. Then the bell would ring and we would clatter down the stairs, past the conveyor belt and the carcass room where the Brethrens stripped every last morsel off the bones of cows, through the storeroom of iced buns, Christmas mince pies and English muffins, until I was back in the white sausage roll room.

I was transferred to pies. Simone and I were chatting too much, and it was slowing us down. Like me, Simone's favourite subject had been English. We both hid our diaries underneath our mattresses. But school in general didn't suit her. She flunked maths and science, and was moved to the work-skills class. The other kids in that class were dull-eyed, empty vessels. Simone sparked and flared next to them. The teachers whispered: should she really be there? Isn't it a waste? But her dad didn't want her to move or pay for remedial tutoring. She could go out and support her more beloved half-brothers and sisters, fruit of the new wife. If Simone's mother were still alive, maybe it would have been different. Her dad hit her. Her stepmother didn't stop him; she was jealous of beautiful Simone and her beautiful dead mother. She allowed Simone's dad to believe that it was Simone who stole the housekeeping money and watered down the gin, not her own children. She blamed Simone for the broken window and curdled milk. But Simone didn't tell me this: this is how I hypothesised the bruises, floating on her skin surface like dead leaves.

The girls on the pie conveyor belt were hard. They didn't have a radio singing them songs as they worked. I missed the nostalgia that surged when Naked Eyes sang, 'Always something there to remind me.' The two sisters who controlled the speed of the conveyer resented my university-educated presence. They accentuated the cigarette crimp in their lips and ramped up the dial forcing each pie into its condom, searing them shut with a heat clamp. The pies were spat out and spun around on a lazy susan. I had to grab two in each hand and stack them in the plastic crates. Every so often they would change the plastic wrapper and there would be a break. There were plain packets and expensive fancy packets — mushrooms suddenly sautéed, onions miraculously caramelised. But they both contained the same pies.

'Fuckin' hurry up, bloody varsity bum,' either one of the sisters would say to me. They slagged off previous workers for being useless and slow, and they were inventorying my shortcomings for later. I would fluster a little more, bursting the pastry casings as I tiled them in their crates.

Dougal picked up a pie, its innards dangling like bad special effects. I was transferred again, first to the custard square station, glooping custard across the metre-square base with a vacuum cleaner pump, and then to the frozens section. He talked as he led me away, not mentioning my repeated failures.

'I really got into religious studies,' he said. 'Even fancied myself doing a masters. Got me thinking about what makes people tick. But I broke up with a girl the night before my first exam, so I went out and got drunk instead of studying. I probably could have applied for an aegrotat, but I had a bit of a crisis — thought it was a sign from God or something. When my results came through, my bro offered me a job. Good money, a bit of responsibility. I'm also on my feet all the time. I couldn't stand a desk job.'

My frozens section co-worker was a sour man, who shared both first names and appearances with Malcolm McDowell from *A Clockwork Orange*. He had a kid and a wife, whom he hadn't spoken to since she had acquired a rose tattoo three weeks earlier to celebrate a darts win. He alphabetised unwanted baked goods and packed frozen sausage rolls with roughened red hands, pointing out the white patches on pastry. That was freezer burn.

The sausage roll wrappers seemed bathed in light from where I worked. Every afternoon the roller door opened into burly Larry's truck, and Lisa, Simone, Bo and Denise took turns flirting and pushing the towers up his ramp. I had been jealous of Larry's freedom; now I was jealous of theirs. Why had I thought it was so bad? I hadn't known better. They waved at me, and later, when they ran out of sausage rolls, Simone and Lisa came over.

'Where have you been? We've been missing you.' They rolled their eyes at Malcolm and he snarled at them, his lip rising to reveal a yellowing canine.

'Buzz off, girls. Can't you see we're busy?'

Lisa and Simone giggled. 'Hey, Rachel, we're going out tonight. You want to come?' Lisa asked.

'Lisa's given her man the flick and she wants to find a new one. Already!' said Simone.

'Uh, sure. That would be fun.'

'Well, here's my address. Come over after dinner and we'll get ready together. Have a few bourbons.'

'Okay.' I didn't really like bourbon. I usually drank cask wine, or bottles of six dollar port.

'Then we'll go nightclubbing. We'll go down to Nite Eyz.'

'Great.' I was nineteen, not quite legal. I wondered whether I needed fake ID.

I clocked out and biked home. I kicked my shoes off at the door, picked up a postcard that was sitting on the table.

'Dear Rachel. Having a great time. The baking is really good here especially the empanadas. We go out dancing until 7 o'clock in the morning. When we walk home it's light. I have made lots of friends and they all laugh at how bad my Spanish is even though I have a Spanish name. A girl called Sandra likes me. See ya, Pablo.'

The cat purred against my legs, licking mince off its lips. I tore the postcard in half and put it in the rubbish bin. Then I changed my mind and fished it out, piecing it together with electrical tape and placing it on the mantelpiece. The streets of Buenos Aires now had a fat red stripe through them.

Now that I was home, I didn't really want to go out again. But if Pablo had found Sandra, then surely I could find someone too. I showered the meaty smells off me, put on a nice dress and convinced my mother to drive me to the part of town where the state houses curled into crescents and cul-de-sacs.

I felt strange in Lisa's little unit. It was different from my family's middle-class bungalow, or the arty student flats where I visited my friends. My friends delighted in their central-city villas, with their inevitably broken sash windows and piles that sank into the soil as if in Pisa. Their halls were showcases for protest and theatre posters, their toilets were wallpapered with movie fliers.

Lisa and her ex had chosen low maintenance over character. Lisa had a velvet painting of a tiger, and a leopard-print rug on her bed. She wore fluffy slippers around the house, and when I arrived she was teasing her frizz into a golden halo. The room smelt of hairspray and air freshener, masking stale cigarette smoke. There were gaps where appliances used to be. A dust-free, stereo-shaped square. A pile of crumbs instead of a toaster. 'He even took my hair iron, the arsehole. He thought it was good for doing the collars of his shirts.' He had left Lisa with the collection of novelty salt and pepper shakers, and the dog, a fluffy white thing that seemed to sit wherever you were about to sit, and whose bottom was stained yellow.

We took a taxi to the nightclub. Although it was midnight it was quiet enough to choose a booth. Three boys were in the booth next to ours and, after conferring, they asked us to dance. I got the short one, his pimples chasing his hairline backwards. Lisa got the tall, muscular one. Simone got the sensitive one with the dark eyes, the one I would have liked, until I discovered they were army boys. Shorty kept brushing his crotch against my thigh, and I danced backwards until I hit a chair. At the end of the song I excused myself and hid in the booth. I sipped my piña colada, tracing the table graffiti with my fingernail.

Why had I come? Dust was the main dancer, and the lights belonged to empty suburban streets without a sweaty crowd to bounce off. There was no urgency, no clash of sweat and aftershave, nothing to challenge Pablo's Buenos Aires. The club would shut soon. There would be no walking home at seven in the morning, slingback heels in hand.

I was relieved when Simone joined me.

'I can't go giving that poor bloke ideas,' she giggled. 'I'm taken.'

We sat together, trying to make conversation over the too-loud music. I nodded a lot; I wanted to give the impression I was a good listener. Dougal was just so different, I think she said. She was knitting him a jersey. Green, to go with his eyes. He was caring. None of the men she had met up until now had been anything like that. What about my ex?

Oh, he was sensitive all right. Far too much so. The slightest thing I'd say would cause offence. He was scared of dogs and let one tear my skirt off rather than rescue me. He didn't much like spiders and would squash them, even though I told him it was bad luck. I didn't think I missed him.

'Look at Lisa — boy, she's fast.' Simone dug me in the ribs. She giggled again. Lisa was raunchy-dancing, shimmying up and down the army boy's pectoral muscles. He had his hand on her butt, flashing between her short skirt and long boots. Her hair glowed in the light, a moon orbiting the disco ball planet. 'Maybe we should leave her to it. I told Dougal I'd go round to his place if it wasn't too late.'

'Should we talk to Lisa? Maybe she wants to go too.'

'Are you kidding? I think she's going to stay for a while.'

I rang my mother from the phone by the coat check, and Simone rang Dougal. We waited on the street below, shivering slightly, even though it was the middle of summer. My mother and Dougal pulled up in their cars at the same time, and I thought about how wrong it all was, how I was a grown woman who should have a man to collect her. I should have at least called a taxi. Dougal winked and waved at me as I climbed into the passenger seat. I tried not to sink down too low. I waved back.

'Who's that?' asked my mother. 'He seemed like a nice man.'

'He is.'

Back in the freezer room the radio played REM. Before I started the job I was a fan. I had even bought the album. Now it sat in my pile of things to trade. 'Would you believe, they put a man on a spoon,' Malcolm sang. He had a good voice, but still.

'Shut up.'

'What did you just say?' Suddenly his eyes were fierce, his eyebrows were quills. 'Did you just tell me to shut up?'

'I was talking to myself,' I said, backtracking.

'Go out with the girls and think you belong around here?' I could feel his spittle on my neck. 'Well, you don't. And those girls are sluts. So don't get above your station. I'll fucking sing if I want to.'

I retreated into myself, biting my lip so that I wouldn't cry. It didn't help. I tipped my head on the side so my tears didn't run down the cheek facing him.

'Hey, that was fun on Friday,' said Lisa, doing her daily rounds of the factory.

'Yeah, you looked like you were enjoying yourself.' I stroked my neck in the place where Lisa's was bruised.

'Oh, that. Turns out that Shaun was a pretty good kisser. But I'm taking things slow this time. And besides, he made me turn off my Judas Priest and he pulled out one of his lame-arse Michael Bolton tapes. I'm not sure if I could be with a man who didn't like Judas.' She waved and she was off. I was alone again with scowling Malcolm.

The next weekend I went around to see Maddie and Renée, friends from university. We drank green ginger wine mixed with cask wine. Dominic the Goth was also there, his wrists clinking with coiled forks, his rings bejewelled with kewpie doll heads. He promised to make Maddie an eyeball choker. Her round cheeks flushed with pleasure. She wanted to open a shop filled with punk clothes and witchcraft supplies, and she was hoping to stock his jewellery.

We roamed the darkening streets, and Renée, the skinniest one among us, slid inside the epilepsy clothing bin. She procured a daisy tablecloth and an indoor bowling T-shirt. Maddie told us how she had seen Rob shooting up morphine. Dominic told us how a girl had presented him with a used tampon in a matchbox. Renée told us she was a lesbian and was looking for a girlfriend. Dominic looked crushed, yet excited. We knew he hung around because of Renée. Nobody was interested in my factory stories.

We padded the effects of excessive drinking with chips from the shop that deep-fried with vegetable oil. We made Dominic get his fish wrapped in a separate packet so we weren't contaminated. Later we went to see Rob perform at Nodule. To express his rage at his father, erratic morphine supplies and supermarket queues, Rob smashed a wall of televisions with a sledge-hammer. Then he smoked a cigarette in his belly button. We slam-danced around in our heavy boots until we were sweaty and bruised, then we stumbled back to Maddie's villa. She made us a cup of earl grey tea and put on *My Bloody Valentine*. All four of us lay on Maddie's bed, eye-tracing the ceiling vines. I wondered whether Renée fancied me now that she was gay. She had a fizz, a new magnetic quality about her. I lay on my hand to stop it from touching her hair.

Maddie lit a roach, reversing it so it burnt within her mouth. She jettisoned the smoke between Renée's lips, brushing them with her own. Then they kissed.

'What happened to the joint?' Dominic asked. He looked really angry. 'What happened to the fucking joint? Did she swallow it?'

I shrugged. So Maddie had noticed it too.

Things became more brittle in the frozens department, and I was suffering from seasonal affective disorder. I only had another couple of weeks to go, but each minute seemed to gape, accommodating dark thoughts about

Pablo and Sandra. Malcolm yelled at me to hurry up, called me a stupid bitch for shattering a box of frozen pies. He was reprimanded by Patrick, but he snarled that he didn't give a shit what that pussy-whipped cunt had to say; I was a stupid bitch, and that was all there was to it.

When I was moved back to the sausage roll line I was grateful. Simone and I resumed our conversations. She let me sniff the swatch of jasmine perfume she was considering buying. It smelt how she should. We gossiped about the Brethren wives that sometimes came by. They were married to the butchers in arranged weddings, and all looked the same in denim skirts, checked shirts and headbands, the ends of their never-cut hair ragged. Denise stood silent, unmoved, in the spot she had occupied for the past seven years. Bo brought in a big bag of green gages and insisted we try them. They were delicious. Each day she had to stretch a little further to wrap the sausage rolls. Lisa thrilled us with updates on her new boyfriend. He took her on motorbike rides and together they burnt his Michael Bolton tapes. He came to collect her one evening in a Metallica T-shirt. He was going to teach her how to shoot a gun.

'You should come round to Dougal's place for dinner before you leave,' Simone said, laying a ribbon of sausage meat across the hot wire that cut the plastic wrap. 'You're vegetarian, right?' She scraped the meat off the wire and sucked her fingernail.

'Yeah,' I said. The pies still taunted me.

'Dougal's a really good cook; I'm sure he can manage vegetarian.'

'Great. I look forward to it.' If only Dougal were mine.

The dinner invitation was issued for my last day.

There was an afternoon tea for the two departing students (there had been five at the beginning of the holidays) and it was catered for with a random assortment of factory grabs and a few bottles of Fanta. The only people who showed any enthusiasm for the farewell were the sausage roll wrappers, but the remaining staff grabbed the elongated break. The cigarette smokers fidgeted. There wasn't a card or a gift, but the eye-patched factory manager thanked us for our hard work, and then went on to announce some positive changes in leave entitlement. This party wasn't about me. I had touched each work station lightly, and although three months felt like a decade, the permanent staff knew it was only a quarter of a year.

We went to Dougal's after we clocked out. Three across his ute, Simone in the middle. The rancid factory smells wafted, even though we had changed our clothes in the locker room before we left. We drove down the main street, past Maddie's flat, past the dairies and the lines of phoenix palms. We drove over the bridge and out of town, the sun setting behind us. I wondered what my friends would be doing, whether they would be cracking open the green ginger wine yet, whether they would be planning another revolution over a freshly rolled joint. I wondered whether Renée and Maddie would kiss again. We turned down an unsealed road and drove along the bank of the river. The tree leaves were supersaturated lime green in the dusk, and the sweet, mosquito-pricked air flooded the car. We passed clumps of exotic lilies, orange tongues protruding from gold petals. The sheep formed hanks, knitting themselves together to sleep.

We turned down Dougal's drive. On the washing line

hung a carcass. 'Oh yeah, I did some home-kill last night.'

We got out of the car, removing our gunky shoes at the door of his bungalow. We walked in through the kitchen, and then into the living room. Dougal offered us a drink and I grabbed a beer, even though I didn't really like it. The walls were rough wood and the floors were polished. There was a giant fireplace around which the sofas were squared. The window framed hills bronzed by sunset. Dougal busied himself in the kitchen, while Simone showed me the green jersey she was knitting: a chunky cable-knit for the winter.

Dougal was a very good cook. He had made fresh flour tortillas and spicy sweet peppers, and sharp salsa and creamy guacamole. I marvelled that a man who worked in a meat pie factory could so easily impress a vegetarian. He said he normally made barbecued chicken to go with it, but he thought it worked well without it. We chatted about the music we liked, and our secret artistic ambitions. I told them how Pablo was due home soon, and how I didn't know what would happen when he returned. I then moved on to Renée, who had occupied my mind lately.

'It's so funny that she's become a lesbian,' I said. 'My friend Maddie told me Renée had been sexually abused by her father. I think he even went to prison for it. I wonder if that's why she's gone off men.'

It was suddenly quiet. The openness about Dougal and Simone's faces withdrew, like touched snail antennae. Dougal scrunched his forehead.

'It's not cause and effect,' said Dougal. 'Some people just are gay. And just because you're abused doesn't mean you're going to start batting for the same team.'

'Maybe not,' I said. I noticed that Simone wasn't saying anything, that she concentrated on mopping up juices with her tortilla. I had a vision of Simone being abused herself. Is that what she implied along the sausage roll line? Had she revealed this secret to Dougal? Had I just made a major faux pas, stumbled upon the root of all of Dougal and Simone's sexual problems, the reason that Simone was academically stunted despite her shining intelligence?

I flushed red and cleared my throat, trying to think of something else to talk about. Were they going to go to any of the concerts in the park? There were just a few weeks of summer left; I heard that there were some good bands playing. And then I started complaining about my neglected record collection, how my boyfriend had left me with all this vinyl and no player. That's when Dougal remembered that he had a spare record player in his garage, and I could have it if I liked, as he now only played CDs.

After coffee and ice cream, Dougal drove me home. Simone was tired; she wanted to go to bed. Things were stilted in the car — the trip over the bridge took forever. I thanked Dougal for the record player and the meal, and he instructed me about needles and amplifiers until the conversation petered out.

'Goodbye, thanks for everything,' I said as I climbed out of the car. I didn't want this to be the end. But I couldn't figure out how to make it last any longer.

Pablo returned from Argentina bearing gifts and a slight pot belly. A woven bag, some strings of beads and a carved stone. A picture of Sandra, plump and scared in her sixteenth-birthday outfit. She wouldn't sleep with him unless they were engaged, and Pablo was too young for that.

I took some seducing. I had become accustomed to solitariness, and the possibilities that it offered me. I moved to Wellington with the factory wages I had saved for fees and rent. I made him follow me. I insisted he learn how to make tortillas with sweet peppers, but they never tasted as good as Dougal's. I made him throw away his record player; my one was better. The diamond cut a clean line through each song.

I graduated at the end of the year with my arts degree. I was semi-unemployed with the rest of my English literature-enriched friends, who had also drifted to Wellington. Pablo was frustrated by my poverty: he had found a job as a computer programmer and couldn't understand why people didn't want my English degree. He wasn't going to subsidise me. I was to be grateful as he slid my photocopied CVs across the café table, as I stole a spoonful of his hard-earned chocolate cake. He left me again, and this time he went to Barcelona.

I rang Renée. She was living with her girlfriend and wasn't available to answer questions about my sexuality. She suggested I meet up with some friends of hers instead.

I was too shy to phone. I got a job at a café. Maddie got a job in a call centre and then got married. Rob overdosed on hard drugs. Dominic discovered the Celestine Prophecies and started setting crystals on leather strings. People were inexplicable and complex, taking offence at seemingly irrelevant things. Nothing seemed as straightforward as it had in my lectures, where effects followed causes.

I ran into Dougal and Simone when I returned home to visit my mother for the weekend. They were in the town square, both wearing green cable-knit jerseys. Yes, they were still at the factory. Lisa had left — they hadn't heard from her in a while. Bo had had a little girl. Dougal still lived in the country, and Simone had moved in — to save on petrol.

And me? Oh, you know, keeping busy.

Simone didn't look damaged. She seemed pleased to see me. But it felt as if this would be the last time we would speak. Next time we might wave. Then we would just walk past each other as if we had never met.

Tilda's mahogany bureau
purses its lips at its mouthful
of filmy underwear and pulp fiction romances.

PLUM JAR

'Blast!' Dorothy has cut her finger halving a black doris and her blood is the same colour as the plum flesh. She knows she should throw this one away, but surely after the boiling and the bottling the blood will lose its potency, leaving a faint sediment of iron on the base of the pot.

It's the bench's fault. It is too low — built for her tiny mother-in-law, with her neat small movements, her precision with peeling and boning and needlepoint. Her mother-in-law had a head of curls secured by a cloche hat, and she was perfectly happy in this kitchen. She didn't stand at the window staring dolefully at her son and daughter, who, with each push of the swing, offload more fruit from the tree. The plums' insistence on being preserved weighs her down like stones in her pockets.

Dorothy has suggested to Douglas that they get the kitchen remodelled, but he doesn't like the idea of money being spent on such things. 'It served my mother well,' he says. Dorothy is not allowed to change much in this house that he was born in, even though Tilda has been dead for three years now. Tilda's mahogany bureau purses its lips at its mouthful of filmy underwear and pulp fiction romances. Tilda's cuckoo clock yells at her to cheer up for the sake of the children.

She didn't think she could miss a place for so long. It has been ten years, but still she craves the movie theatres, the libraries, the corner stores with their ice creams, their loaves of bread so effortlessly procured. Here she has to make her own, except on Thursdays when it is grocery day. That is when she loads the kids into the car and they spat over the gravel roads, through the windy hills, behind the tractors and the flocks of sheep ushered by farmers and dogs, until they arrive in town, forty-five minutes later.

After the grocery shopping, she goes to the library to borrow gardening and home-decorating books that can sit proudly on her bedside table. Then she slips into Antonio's Gently Loved Books to buy the romances for her disapproving bureau. She sells the ones she has read during the previous week to the second-hand bookseller (Antonio?), who greets her by name. 'Why hello, Dorothy, lovely to see you lighting up my shop. The standard issue, is it?'

His dark hair is smoothed back with Brylcreem; a smile or a frown of scar descends from the patch over his left eye, a smile or a frown depending on which side you look at him from. Instead of a parrot he has a terrier, who wears a different knitted jacket each time Dorothy sees him. Today he is asleep in his window basket, cocooned in orange acrylic.

PLUM JAR

Sometimes Antonio presses the likes of *Wuthering Heights*, *Madame Bovary* and *Dangerous Liaisons* upon her, insisting that they are the real thing. But they are dense and their language is old-fashioned, demanding attention she does not have to spare.

She wonders what her life would have been like if she had married the bookseller instead of her limping husband, bookkeeper to the more able-bodied farmers and fishermen and timber millers who live in the surrounding countryside. Would the bookseller have torn off her negligee, ribboned the fabric to tie her wrists to the bedposts? Or would she have been pinned beneath his bulk, making To Do lists and remembering song lyrics as he went about his business?

Today is Thursday, and after she has stewed her plums in a light syrup she will sterilise her jars. They will jostle and clink in the big tin pot, and then she will almost fill them with dark clots of plums. She will ladle syrup over the top, wipe with a cloth and cover with a metal seal, screwing the band tightly. She will leave them to cool as she makes that journey to town, her children administering Chinese burns to each other in the back seat.

'You should join the book club,' the bookseller suggests as she hands over her three romances wrapped in newspaper. 'What did you do to your finger?'

Dorothy looks down to see that the blood has seeped through the bandage. 'I cut it this morning. Get down from there!' she yells to her kids, who are climbing onto the elephant foot-stool and pulling books from the top shelf.

'Oh, leave them. I don't mind. Just some dusty old

atlases that nobody ever wants to buy.'

'Atlases? I love those. Only they make me feel sad, seeing all the places I've never had a chance to visit.'

'That's why you should join the book club. You can do a bit of armchair travelling. The meetings are here, the last Thursday of every month, after I shut up shop. This month we're reading a great book by this American girl, Sylvia Plath. She was married to Ted Hughes — you should read his poetry. She killed herself the same year it was published; she put her head in her gas oven. Rumour has it the babysitter was meant to turn up and rescue her, but she was late. I'll lend it to you if you like. Take it home and read it and tell me if you want to come along.'

'All right,' Dorothy says, a little unsurely, tracing the silver foiled letters. *The Bell Jar*.

The book is at the bottom of the laundry basket, and after she has folded every item and put it in its rightful place, she is allowed to open it. The children have gone to bed, and she has placed the remains of the casserole in the fridge, washed up the custard and apple crumble pudding plates, and left them to drain in the rack. She doesn't enjoy cooking, even though it is what she spends most of her time doing. She supposes it's the subject matter; she wonders whether she would feel differently about it if she were allowed to make a pasta carbonara, a bouillabaisse, But Douglas is quite set in his ways: a meal is not a meal without a potato.

The children follow his lead, turning up their noses when she offers them something new, and each has a quirk, her daughter stringing a necklace of carrot slices around the edge of her plate, and her son refusing fish.

Every night she forces herself to slice the onions and brown the meat; every night she gets out the sago or the rice or the custard powder. She can't help but hurt herself when she cooks, and there seems to be a pattern to it. Three cuts, three burns, then a pot dropped onto a toe. She wonders whether she is doing it on purpose, but when it happens she is still shocked as if it's the first time.

The book crackles when she opens it, and the ink rises from the page in a chemical waft. If she presses her nose to the flysheet she can smell the bookseller — his tobacco and dog fur, his musk. Douglas looks at her over his newspaper, and she returns the book to her knee.

It is smooth for something worthy — easier to read than the other books she has been given. Esther is in New York, somewhere Dorothy has always wanted to go, and she has an internship with a magazine. It's such a glamorous, improbable scenario that it makes her ache. Dorothy's father made her leave school when she was fourteen — the family was hard up and she had to work in an office, typing for tuppence — but when she could still dream, Dorothy was going to be a reporter in a tailored tweed suit, her sharp, probing pencil bisecting her bun. Dorothy recognises Esther's detachment. Dorothy's body cooks and cleans, but she floats above, her mind the helium to fill a balloon. She wonders if one day her hand will let go of the string.

'What are you reading, dear?' Douglas asks her.

'Oh, just something for my book club.' She holds the cover up.

'A book club? Well, it's nice that you've decided to join something. My mother always got involved in the community. The gardening club, the church committee, the Ladies' Auxiliary. Just as long as it doesn't take you away from the children.'

His mother, his damned mother. Even dead and buried she still exerts control. And the children, well, he's never there for them. When he is home he is wrapped up, a parcel of rustling paper.

'Actually, I'll be late home next Thursday. I have my first meeting at 5.30.'

'Oh.' He looks disconcerted. Dorothy is always there, however reluctantly. 'Well, I expect you'll leave dinner in the oven for me. But what will the children do? They'll be tired and hungry by the time they get home.'

'They can stay with Marjorie. They'll enjoy spending some time with their cousins. And Marjorie is a very good cook.' Dorothy hasn't actually asked Marjorie yet. She is nervous: Marjorie will pry, perhaps sniff out a betrayal, or the intention of one. She will also demand a social visit in return, and Dorothy will have to listen to her prattle about school sports and ageing parishioners. She will mention her daily social interactions, and Dorothy will feel lonely and isolated. Dorothy can only remark to strangers about the unseasonable balmy weather.

Dorothy has lined up her jars in the window. The light turns them into stained-glass windows. Her children skid on their bicycles, making half-moons of dirt in the gravel. This upsets Douglas, but she can't stop them. That would involve suggesting another activity. She hasn't the energy to make them to do their homework. She is hypnotised by the variance in plum tones, and she wants to dive into the bottle, sliding among their voluptuous forms.

'Mum? Mum, are you okay?'

PLUM JAR

Dorothy starts. She must have dozed off. It is her daughter, tugging on her sleeve.

'Mum, when will dinner be ready?' Dorothy looks at the clock. It is 5.45pm, a time when normally everything is simmering on the stove, prepared for the six o'clock return of Douglas.

'Oh. Oh dear. Soon, love. I just got a little bit distracted.'

The bookshop door is open slightly, even though the sign says Closed. It tinkles as she enters, and a silhouette at the top of the stairs appears, saying, 'Come on up. Flick the lock behind you: you're the last one to arrive.'

Well, it wasn't easy getting away from Marjorie. She had heard things about the bookseller — his lothario ways, his denizen of sin at the top of the stairs, his propensity for banned pieces of literature. She was still shouting tidbits at Dorothy as she walked down the path, away from the house.

Dorothy climbs the steps, conscious of her disadvantage in light. Her face is open and illuminated, whereas the bookseller remains a dark, hulking figure.

'Welcome, welcome, Dorothy.'

'Hello, Antonio,' she says.

'Tony,' he corrects. The stairs creak at her discomfort.

She enters a hall and there he is, without the barrier of the counter. He is shorter than she thought: about her height. He must serve customers on a podium. He is wearing a burgundy dressing gown, the gold cord unravelling.

The other ladies are already seated, two languidly on a sofa and another sprawled on a pile of cushions. There is something loose about them; she wonders if they are bra-burners.

'A sherry? A glass of wine?' Antonio asks.

'Water is fine for me.'

He smiles and moves towards the kitchen.

'Oh Tony, you can't let her get out of it that easily. Bring her a glass of wine.'

'No, I'd prefer a sherry, actually,' Dorothy says. Maybe it would help. She looks around for a place to sit. All that remains is a two-seater, and she knows that if she sits there, Tony will sit beside her: a terrifying prospect, even though she has imagined him stretching his hand over the counter to take hers.

He brings it to her in a tumbler, not the small cut-crystal glass she was expecting.

'It's how they drink it in Barcelona,' he explains, noting her confusion. She takes a small sip and puckers; it is not as sweet as she is accustomed to.

Tony sits down, and the springs confer in the middle of the sofa. Dorothy tenses her thigh muscles and presses firmly into the carpet with her feet to prevent herself from sliding into his ravine.

'So, ladies, what did we think of Ms Plath's book?'

The women look at one another and giggle, a flutter of nerves and coquetry. Who will start? Who will say something first?

'I found it very powerful,' says the woman in the caftan with the Cleopatra eyes.

'Thank you, Samantha, and how did you find it so?'

'Just that account of depression, you know. I never really understood why my grandmother used to go away on "holidays", it was all so hush-hush. Her last trip, she never came back. And then there was the funeral, and nobody could settle on how she died. But this — it kind of gave me some understanding of why.'

'What do you mean, why?' says the woman with a mushroom cloud of hair and tight corduroy trousers. 'This girl is so self-indulgent; she's got no reason to be depressed. A trip to New York, looks, no need to go on a diet: I think she needs to pull herself together and stop wasting our time. I'm sorry, this book was so cold, I couldn't feel anything but irritation for her.'

'Thank you, Marion,' says Tony. 'And what about you, Donna? What did you think of the book?'

Donna is the most languorous and slightly plump, sprawled across the cushions in chiffon. 'I liked the bit about the figs. Remember, where she's trying to decide what to do in life, and there are too many choices, and she feels overwhelmed? And as she tries to decide, the figs start rotting and fall on the ground? I felt like that when I was younger. I still don't know whether I picked the right fig!' Donna giggles.

Tony nods sagely, stroking his chin. 'What about you, Dorothy?'

Dorothy is thinking about her fig tree. The fruit were just formed, their seeds still creamy, when her father took out his axe. She feels a flash of resentment at Donna for even having a choice. Who are all these women? They seem so bold.

'Um, I think I'll just listen for now.'

And she listens to them talk about Doreen's willingness to sleep with so many men.

'I was a bit like that when I was at university,' says Marion.

'You still are,' retorts Samantha.

She listens as they discuss Esther's hemorrhaging at the loss of her virginity, and the overwhelming physicality of Buddy.

'I was like a stuck pig my first time,' says Samantha.

'Samantha, we're in mixed company,' says Donna.

'Oh yeah,' says Samantha, glancing at Dorothy, not Tony.

She listens as they remark on Esther's hatred of her mother. 'But does she really hate her? Or is she just saying that?' says Donna.

'*I* hate my mother,' says Marion.

'What do you make of this quote?' asks Tony. "*I've gone around for most of my life as in the rarefied atmosphere under a bell jar.*" Plath apparently wrote that in a letter.'

'Sounds like she needs to get out more,' says Marion. 'And what is she talking about? She got to go to New York. The furthest I've been is Wellington.'

'I think she feels suffocated by her life,' says Dorothy. And then the room is quiet as all eyes turn towards her. Suddenly her voice sounds tremulous and she doesn't want to go on; she is sure to make a fool out of herself.

'Yes, Dorothy?' Tony prompts.

Dorothy continues, nervously. 'I think that all the expectations, all those people wanting her to do certain things, be a certain somebody, well, it makes it difficult for her to breathe. I think she feels as though she can't escape, and the only way out is to take all those pills and crawl under the house and die.'

'Very well put, Dorothy.'

And Dorothy smiles, her cheeks thrumming with blood, but all she can think about among that clattering echo of words misused are her plums, and that thuck sound as the seal sucks the air out of the jar, the metal ring clattering against the glass.

'Is it treat time yet, Tony?' asks Donna.

'Certainly,' says Tony. He turns, and as his hip touches Dorothy she jumps. He pulls out a stained cigarette and a box of matches, but when he lights it it doesn't smell like Douglas's tobacco. He passes it to Samantha, who takes a drag and begins to cough, and then passes it to Marion, who holds it, crablike, between her orange-painted nails. Donna inhales next, and her languidness clicks over to the next level: she melts into her cushions like an ice cream dropped onto hot asphalt. She hands it to Dorothy.

'No, I can't.'

'Why not?' asks Donna. 'It'll make you feel groovy.'

'I — it's just, oh, my, look at the time. I have to go and pick up the children.'

She stands quickly. It is clear that she is not one of them. As bohemian as they are, they did not feel so bereft when they finished the book. Dorothy gathers up her things. Her purse, her keys. 'Thank you, Tony,' she says.

'Any time, Dorothy. I'll give you the book for the next meeting when you come by the shop.' He stands and kisses her on the cheek.

Dorothy blushes. She tries to kiss him in return but her lips only hit air.

'Nice to meet you,' Samantha calls out, and then dissolves into giggles. The others begin to giggle too, and Dorothy has the sensation that she is in the schoolyard again, being laughed at for her patched woollen skirt, which she wore every day that winter.

When she arrives at Marjorie's she finds her children hunched over a puzzle, mugs of cocoa next to them. They are speaking softly to each other: a rare display of unity. They confer over the elbows and sockets of each piece, arranging a Fachwerk house within a gingerbread landscape. Marjorie's children are on the floor, a sheet of ply laid out in front of them, an even more epic puzzle being worked on.

'Hello,' she says.

They turn, they brighten; she is surprised that they do that when she feels like such a robot of a mother.

'Mum!' they cry. 'Look how far we've got!'

'Very good,' she hears herself say. 'Aren't you clever?'

They are pleased with themselves and refocus on the task, determined to plug the gaps before they are bundled into the car.

The trip across the gravel road lulls them to sleep and, one at a time, she carries them into the house. Her lame husband cannot help. She walked across the marital threshold on her own two feet. As she tucks the children into bed she is flooded with love, and guilt that this is the time when she loves them the best.

In the kitchen Dorothy opens a jar of plums. There are fresh ones in the fridge — she knows she is plundering her winter supplies. She plops three onto her plate. They slide around the bowl and she has to secure them with a fork to spoon off the flesh. The plums are tart; they shock her. She sucks each stone and the rough edges scratch her tongue.

'Dorothy?' Her husband is at the door, leaning into the frame to take the weight off his gammy leg. 'Are you coming to bed?'

'No,' she says. She spoons three more plums into her bowl. She extracts her romance from under the teatowels. She overwrites Douglas's presence with creamy breasts and cruel upper lips.

Douglas stands fast, his bulk creaking the wood. 'Did you enjoy the book club?'

Dorothy sighs. 'I'm not sure.'

'I had trouble heating up my dinner. It dried out a little bit.'

'That's a shame.'

'Do you think you will be going again?'

'Yes,' says Dorothy. 'Yes, I think I will.'

'Well, I'm sure I'll get the knack of it. Or I suppose I could make myself a sandwich. What's that you're reading?'

'Goodnight, Douglas.' Dorothy spits a stone into her bowl.

'Goodnight.'

And as the heroine offers a stretch of porcelain neck, Douglas shuffle-thuds down the hall.

Who wants to talk
to a girl with her
mouthfull of
shrimp?
Mingling is the name
of the game.

Notes on ETIQUETTE

1. Janice cleans her nails with her silver hairclip. They are gritty from when she plunged her forefinger and thumb into the window box of ranunculus to extract a half-smoked cigarette. She had buried it when she heard her buzzer ring last night, and as Peter had climbed the ninety-three steps to her apartment she had executed a dance of the seven veils to shoo away the smell of smoke. She had been so pleased with herself for going without cigarettes for a four-martini date that she had thrown the rest of her Marlboro Lights into the bin outside the corner deli.

'You coulda just handed them to me,' called the local homeless guy after her swing of straight brown hair. 'Saved my arm from this filthy trash.'

Janice balls up the grit and flicks it onto the floor-boards. She slides the clip back into her hair and looks at herself in the mirror. She knows she isn't really this way — that her sucked-in cheeks and cocked eyebrows slacken as soon as she turns away — but this arrangement is more pleasing, more Garbo. She wonders how Peter first saw her. Whether he found her striking or odd. Toby, her ex-boyfriend, told her she looked like a horse, that blue blood meant inbred. He swiped her father's ring off her bureau, saying she wouldn't miss it — she had too much. But she does miss it. Like she misses her father. By the time she got hold of Toby's new cell number, calling from a phone box so he couldn't ID her and refuse to answer, he had already pawned it and spent the money on a rare R. Crumb comic.

Janice lights the cigarette. It tastes earthy, but she hasn't watered her windowbox in a while, so it isn't damp. She wonders whether Peter is going to call her today. She doesn't think so; she knows the three-days-post-date phone rule. But still, they had so much to say to each other, poised like lemon slices on the rims of their bar stools, scalloping each other's sentences. She wants to talk again. He works in Wall Street, but really he's a filmmaker, and that appeals to her. But although she likes her men a little artsy, a little indy, they're usually the ones who need her money. Peter bought the drinks last night, and even though he didn't accompany her home, she was sure that there was something between them, that he must have a no-sex-on-the-first-date policy even if she doesn't. Damn, why won't he call?

2. 'Swing the golf club a little more. Put your whole body into it,' says Peter.

Janice adjusts her scarf (Hermes, her mother's), straightens her skirt, which has twisted along with her swing, and lifts the golf club again. She pulls in her stomach and smiles at the camera. She knows it's only digital but she feels celluloid. 'Point of etiquette, number two,' she elocutes. 'Quiet. Golf requires a lot of concentration, so don't go chattering across the green. Imagine you're in a library, and the little flags are the librarians with their fingers pressed to their lips. When you're drinking cocktails after the game, that's when you can gossip about Miss Hunter's recent engagement, or Mr Eagleton's new polo horse. Compose your anecdotes for later, and watch this.' The club cracks the dimpled ball into an arc. Janice shields her eyes from the sun and follows its descent into the creek. 'Fuck,' she says.

'CUT!' says Peter. 'That's great. You were hot. I think we got it that time.' He folds up the camera and zippers it into his bag. He pulls Janice towards him and slides his cool hand under her shirt. He puts his other hand down the waistband of her skirt (which has yet again twisted, the zipper running down her belly) and runs his finger around the elastic of her underpants.

'What, here?' says Janice.

'Why not?'

Janice watches as another ball charts the contour of the hill, hits the grass and trickles into the hole. 'Maybe we should go to your place instead.'

'Oh, no. My place is kinda messy. All my equipment and shit.'

'I still haven't seen your place. When are you going to invite me over?'

They are interrupted by the roar of a golf cart carrying a fat white-haired man and a thin white-haired woman. 'Is that a hole in one?' Janice hears the man say. 'I say it is. Look, Sherry, a hole in one!'

'My, aren't you clever,' says Sherry. She pats the whitehaired dog in her Louis Vuitton tote bag. And then the moment is gone.

3. As Janice zips up the pink dress she thinks of Julia Roberts in *Pretty Woman*. Somehow this is making her feel like a whore. Is Peter parodying her, with his oh-so-righteous, Irish-Catholic, I-grew-up-in-the-Bronx stoop? She majored in Irony, sarcasm intersecting cigarette drags in the coffee shop after literature class. Surely she should have some input. The dress he's picked out is nipped in at the waist and has a full skirt, a sweetheart neckline and little capped sleeves. Her jeans and T-shirt have collapsed on the dressing-room velvet stool.

'That's perfect. You look the part. But we need some gloves. White ones.' Peter turns to the shop assistant, and her mascara-laden eyelashes radiate precisely. They don't clump like Janice's. Alone in front of the mirror she picks off a glob and, not knowing where else to put it, she applies it to the inside of her handbag.

'I'm sorry, sir. Why don't you try the glove counter at Saks?'

'Great idea.' Peter takes a sash of hair and wraps it around Janice's forehead. 'What do you think, a little more Hepburn?'

'Absolutely,' says the assistant. '*Breakfast at Tiffany's* is one of my favourite movies.' She winks at Peter, and Janice briefly gets the impression that the assistant has been through all this before.

Janice slumps on the stool in her underwear, her flesh pleating her torso. She's thinking of the time her mother did this to her. Yanked her down from the tree where she was climbing, her shorts peach-stained, her feet tough from bark and gravel. Took her to the department store and dressed her in white, with a lilac ribbon, for the garden party. How she picked her scab in the changing room and bled on the dress, and her mother was angry at having to buy the stained garment. Rita, the maid, plunged the garment into cold water the minute they got home. The rusty blood dispersed. That didn't spare Janice from the slap on her thigh, the supper she refused in the nursery. She regretted the stand at 4am, and sneaked down the stairs for cookies. When she opened the pantry door there was Rita, sitting on the flour bin, sobbing. She started at the sight of Janice, her elbows flew out and knocked cereal packets off the shelf.

'Your father's gone,' she said, a confetti of Rice Bubbles at her feet.

'Where?' asked Janice.

'I don't know where. Ask your mother.' She pulled the pantry door shut between them. Janice crouched down and ate the Rice Bubbles off the floor.

She never wore that white dress, but it haunted her closet. She remembers her mother railing at Rita for not putting plastic baggies around the tags when she washed it so that she couldn't return it. Rita quit after that, and Janice was left to answer the door to guests who hadn't heard that the garden party was off. They spent the rest of the summer alone in the big house, first eating the chicken, the potato salad, the cakes and slices that had been prepared the day before, then moving on to scrambled eggs and beans out of cans. The ring was the only thing Janice managed to keep of her father's, and she put it on a chain around her neck, under her T-shirts so her mother wouldn't see. Rather than packing his clothes in the trunk, they had a bonfire before they returned to the city. Her mother toasted marshmallows over his burning shirts and pants, but Janice refused to eat them. To her they tasted like charred flesh.

'That damn Rita,' her mother said. 'I wish we never hired her, the slut. It was your father who insisted. He wanted a harem, but she wasn't enough for him. Oh god, what did I do to deserve this?'

Janice drew her legs up to her chest and shivered, even though the flames were hot.

'Are you done yet?' calls Peter from the other side. Janice passes the pink dress through the curtain. She sits on the stool until she thinks she can hear the squiggle of his fountain pen on the receipt, then she pulls on her grey and blue faded clothes and follows the pink dress out. 'Why, thank you,' she says as Peter hands her the bag. It is wrapped in mint-green tissue. It rustles.

'To Saks?' asks Peter. 'Or should we stop in for a drink first?'

'A drink would be good.' She fumbles in her bag for a cigarette.

'Do you have to smoke on the street?' says Peter. 'You really should give up.'

She shrugs and returns the cigarette to its pack. He's so uptight about rules that don't even belong to him.

4. 'Point of etiquette number four.' Janice lifts her martini to the camera. 'Don't spend your evening at the buffet table. Who wants to talk to a girl with her mouth full of shrimp? Mingling is the name of the game.'

She stretches out her hand. 'How do you do? Handshakes must be firm and dry. Smile, but discreetly check your teeth first to make sure you don't have cracker crumbs stuck in them. Say the person's name, and remember it. Say a little rhyme in your head if it helps. Like Nancy Gnocchi Nose. Don't stay too long — mingle and tingle. A girl must maintain an air of mystery. Excuse yourself after a few minutes and introduce yourself to someone else.' Janice turns her head a little, takes a sip of the martini. She spins to show the tulle underskirt of her new dress.

'That's great, hon. You're a natural. This is going so much quicker than usual.' Peter puts down his camera and slumps into Janice's salvaged hair-setting chair. He slurps at the martini that has been waiting for him, and pulls out the olive before he's even made it halfway through. 'And this apartment has such fantastic light.'

'What do you mean, quicker than usual? Have you done this before?'

'No, no, no. Of course not. I mean quicker than my usual projects. The *Day at the Races* movie, you'd think that I'd get enough footage in one day, but no, I had to keep on going back again and again. The bookies didn't want to be filmed unless I placed a bet, the ladies pulled their hats down over their faces, I wasn't allowed near the horses and then my battery ran down when I came across a male jockey who looked just like the young Elizabeth Taylor. It was a nightmare.' He takes another slurp of his martini and looks at his watch. 'Oh shit, is that the time? I gotta go; I'm meant to be meeting some friends.'

'Can I come?' She hasn't met any of his friends yet.

'Uh, I don't know. It's just a group of guys from the

neighbourhood, they're kinda coarse, I don't think you would like them.'

'I like coarse. I'm only fingerbowls and fine china for your camera, Peter.'

'It's a guy thing. They're all married, y'know. They want to go to one of those hooter bars. I don't understand — I'm not into that kinda thing.'

'Whatever. Listen, my mom's coming to town next week. Would you like to meet her?'

'Sure, I'd love to meet your mom. But I might be tied up with work; I can't guarantee anything.'

'So will I see you later?'

'I'll call you.'

'Please do. We haven't even talked.'

'Whaddaya mean? We talked plenty. I got it all here on film.' He smiles, and it's open, tiled with teeth. He kisses Janice on the cheek and slouches, loose-boned, to the door. 'Later.'

Janice wonders what she will say to her mother if he doesn't show. She has offered him to her: her handsome, artistic, financially independent boyfriend who only sometimes makes her feel cheap. After all these years of stoners and garage-band musicians. She knows that her Dartmouth degree, her fluency in French and excellent knowledge of Grecian vases is not enough for her mother's endorsement. But she's sure Peter will tip the balance. He knows how to hold a knife, even if he learnt it in a book.

5. 'So where's your man?' Her mother is immaculately coiffed, in a suit that may be Chanel but will neither confirm nor deny. She has lipsticked her chardonnay in

three different places, and smiles at the waiter who refills her glass. He pours one for Janice and she takes a sip.

'He was going to come. He got called back by work.' And it's true — she met him in his foyer and they walked a couple of blocks together. He looked different in a suit, sober and handsome, and Janice felt like the figurehead of a liner, her cheeks sea sprayed, coursing through an ocean of people. But then his phone rang — some problem with a credit-default swap, he had to get back, millions of dollars were at stake. So here she is, shipwrecked on a bench seat. She washes her tears away with a glass of water. She makes them glide backwards down her throat rather than her cheeks. This way, her mother cannot suggest the name of a good therapist, or barrage her with the you-don't-know-how-lucky-you-are-count-your-blessings bullets.

'Oh, Janice. I was hoping to meet him.'

Janice and *so disappointing* are synonymous in her mother's lexicon. 'That's so disappointing,' she sighed, when Janice announced she wouldn't be going to the prom. 'What a let-down,' she said when she had returned home unexpectedly early to discover Janice and a stoner boyfriend half naked on the living-room floor. 'I had thought you were more sensible than that,' she said, when she broke down the bathroom door to the sound of Janice throwing up her fourth dinner for the week. 'Oh, Janice,' she said when the drugstore rang up to report Janice's theft of a turquoise eyeliner and a roll of chocolate laxatives.

Janice doesn't see why *she's* the one who apparently disappoints. It's not as if her mother has been altogether satisfactory.

'I have some news, darling. I'm getting married again.'

'You are? To whom?'

'Do you remember Bradley? We played tennis doubles together. His wife died of cancer last year, and we've been seeing a little of each other at the club. He's here, actually.'

'Where?'

'Well, I sent him off shopping because I wanted to tell you alone. I'll call him. Tell him to come by.'

'No, don't.' Janice doesn't think she can face her mother's new man when hers has slipped away.

'Oh. All right, but you must meet him before the wedding. I'm here to look at dresses. We thought we'd make it September. When the leaves turn. I'll tell him to make his own plans for lunch.' Her mother fishes in her bag for her phone. 'Have you heard from your father lately?' she asks in her fake casual voice.

'Not since my birthday.' He called from Barcelona; his new wife was the curator at some museum there. He couldn't talk long — the baby was crying, his wailing erasing Janice's voice as if it were chalk on a blackboard. Her father has a new life now, and she's just a lesson he once learned. She had hoped he would invite her over to stay, but he didn't.

'Bradley? Just pick yourself up something for lunch. She's not taking it very well . . . emotionally fragile, yes . . . Yes, I know. At least she's eating, she's filled out a little . . . okay, love you too. Bye, sweetie.' She pulls her earpiece out and holds the phone out long-sightedly to push the end-call button.

'Filled out a little? What, do I look fat?' Janice asks her mother. She snaps the menu shut.

'No, honey, you've just got a little flesh on your bones. It looks good.'

'And what the fuck do you mean, *emotionally fragile*? What about you? You think I don't know where you were when I was at boarding school?'

Her mother's face trembles, but then, as if trained to defuse family spectacles, the waiter appears.

'May I take your order, ma'am?' he says to Janice's mother.

'Why, yes, I'll have the quail salad. But could you please put the dressing on the side?'

6. 'Point of etiquette number six. Bread-and-butter letters,' says Janice. Peter paid for her to have a French polish, and now her normally naked nails are the colour of moonstones. She admires them holding her fountain pen. 'After attending a social function or receiving a gift, one must always compose a letter. Forget about email; the watermarked heavy-wove paper is all part of the deal.'

She presses the nib down, and ink bleeds into the paper. 'Dear Mom,' she writes. 'Thank you for inviting me for lunch. I still haven't forgiven you. I would appreciate a little honesty in our relationship. You say that Dad left because he got himself into a pickle with Rita, but don't you think his cheating was symptomatic rather than causal? The man wanted to study art; you made him study law. Shit, you had enough money to support him, why did you have to turn him into your father? Why are you such a control freak?'

'Cut!' says Peter.

'What did you think?' asks Janice. They didn't

rehearse this, but she wants to be part of the creative process.

'I don't know, Janice. It's a bit heavy. It's not exactly what I had in mind. It's meant to be parody, not daytime soaps.'

'What do you mean, *daytime soaps*? This is my life I'm talking about. I thought you'd appreciate a little bit of revelation.'

'You of all people should understand. You just don't talk about that kind of thing in polite society. You keep that sort of stuff to yourself.'

'What, so you're polite society? Is that why you don't tell me about yourself? Is that why you still haven't invited me over to your apartment? I mean, hell, we've been going out for two months now. I'm beginning to think you might have a room full of your ex-girlfriends' heads.'

'Oh, come on. The reason I haven't invited you over is because it's such a wreck, I'm embarrassed.'

'I don't mind mess.'

Peter looks around, taking in her white bed linen, her red vase with its single orchid stem in it. His eyes run along her rack of neatly hung clothes, and out the window where her geraniums burst from their pots. 'Don't you?'

7. Bar-ce-lo-na, Janice types into Google. Just because her father has neglected to invite her doesn't mean she can't visit. She's wondering whether Peter might like to come with her, so they can hang out in neutral territory, rather than always being around at her place. She knows things are not running smoothly with him. Maybe away from Manhattan, the viewfinder of his

camera, the exclusive camaraderie of his friends, they can start afresh. Throw tomatoes at the running of the bulls. Drink *fino* in a flamenco bar. And she needs to escape her mother, who keeps calling her, importuning her with her wedding plans, wanting Janice to feel included — maybe she could be a bridesmaid? How about reading a Shakespearian sonnet during the ceremony? (Come on, sweetheart, your tutor always said you had dramatic talent.) Tonight she's meeting her mother and Bradley for dinner, and she's dreading it.

'We'll go somewhere fun,' her mother promised. 'How about a tapas restaurant?'

Janice gets 17,800,000 hits. Overwhelming. She Googles her father's name instead. And there he is, featured on the websites of a few dealer galleries. One in Barcelona, one in Paris, one in Brooklyn, NYC, one in Seattle. Wow. He's doing okay. She types in her own name. Nothing, although sites come up for people with the same name. Someone with a PhD in gerontology. A beagle enthusiast. A gestural drawing teacher. She Googles Peter. And there is a similar smattering of pages. An English politician, a blog about death. And what's this: *Notes on Etiquette*? She clicks the link. She goes to a home page dominated by type. *Peter Pike . . . video artist . . . postmodern explorations . . . surveillance* — what the fuck? *Download clips from Peter's latest projects*. She follows this link. And there, is it? Is that her? Swinging the golf club? But it's not just her: underneath the heading *Golf* there are a number of little clips to be played. She clicks on a couple and they pop up in their tiny windows, chirruping. A blonde, anaemic-looking woman with a hooked nose explains the rules of golf. A redhead in a twinset and pearls discusses the finer details of the follow-through. The brunette, who looks just like her, has her fist thrust down the hole to retrieve the ball.

Fuck. He'd said it was for an indie short film. She'd envisaged it debuting at the Tribeca Film Festival, before something ground-breaking and feature length. She'd imagined herself in the *Village Voice*, a break-out box, the new it-girl. How was she so easily duped? Why hadn't she asked more questions? Is this her fault for meeting him through an internet dating site?

She closes the windows, click, click, click, like Pandora, trying to squash all the bad things back into the box. She sees a link for comments underneath each video clip, and next to her name is the number 56, but she doesn't want to read that she's fat or hot or inbred or fuckable. She dials Peter's mobile.

'Hi Janice,' he says. He has allocated a special ring on his phone for her. And she thought it charming.

'I found the site, Peter.' She sounds calm.

There is silence. Then, 'What site?'

'You know what I'm talking about: Peter Pike, video artist. Your *postmodern . . . etiquette . . . surveillance* site.'

'Oh.'

'So, when were you planning on telling me about it?'

'When it was finished. It was going to be a surprise.'

'Really? Don't you need my permission for that kind of surprise? I mean, shouldn't I have signed a model release form or something? It's on the internet for the whole world to see. I could fucking sue you.'

'Uh, your response, it's really interesting to me. Can I swing by your place and film it as part of the project?'

'No. I'm changing my locks. I may even move. What was I, just another standard-issue blue-blood? Wait, are you Bluebeard?'

'No, no, of course not. I like you, Janice. You really stand out. Everyone agrees — did you read the comments?'

'No.'

'Well, you should, you're a star. The other girls, you shoulda read a few of the outa-line messages. Hey, come round to my apartment. I'll clean it up specially.'

'What, are you crazy? I don't ever want to see you again. And you are going to take me off your website or else I'm going to report you to the police.'

'I'm not taking you off. You're an integral part of my project. Don't you want to be famous?'

'Yeah, but not like this. Are you still seeing those other girls? Was sex the part of the project that I need a credit card number to download?'

'Come on, Janice. Don't be like this. Lighten up. Why don't you come out with some of my friends tonight? We're going to that bar on West Twenty-first and Broadway. The one with the red glass windows and the octopuses in tanks. Did you know that octopuses are really smart?'

Janice can't believe what she's hearing. The turnaround makes her feel seasick, pitches her overboard. 'What the fuck? Do I care about this shit?' she yells.

'Well, they are. I heard that they climbed out of their aquariums and arranged the tumblers into a pyramid formation. Now they have to put chicken wire over the top to stop them from escaping.'

'Stop it. Is anything you say real?'

'I'm in hedge funds, what do you think? So are you

going to come?'

'I'm meeting my mom. And you should know, asshole. You always accept the first invitation.'

'Do you want me to come with you? I know you've wanted me to meet your mom for a while.'

'I don't want to see you again. Do you hear me? Of course you're not coming along. Arrgh!'

Janice's head is full of static, her vision a fractured kaleidoscope. She doesn't know how to break the loop so she throws the phone across the room. It hits the brick wall and splits open, revealing its wiry intestines.

She opens her wardrobe, screeching the wire hangers along their rack. She selects a white dress and lays it on the bed. She picks up the phone, gathering the shards of plastic, stuffing the wires back into its hollow cavity. She wonders whether she can glue it back together again. She goes to the computer again to check the address of the restaurant. West Twenty-first Street. At Broadway. Damn.

8. Bradley has had his teeth capped. They are bridal in their whiteness and they contradict the lines on his face. Janice wonders whether he is going to have botox for the wedding. He is fit and taut in a desiccated way, as if none of the sweat he lost in his exercise regime has been replaced, despite his Evian-stocked fridge. Janice wonders whether he is petrified, a fallen tree in the forest. He shakes her hand and his is dry and rough, like bark.

Janice scans the menu, and her mother deflects the waiter with the bread basket. 'No carbs for me, thank you. Not until the honeymoon.'

'But I want carbs. I like bread,' says Janice.

'I can see,' says her mother, casting her eye down Janice's T-shirt-wrapped torso. Then she looks up.

'Hey, Janice.' Janice lurches. Stops herself from adopting the brace position under the table.

It is Peter. Janice's mother smiles.

'I was just passing, on my way to the bar, and I saw you in here.'

'Allow me to introduce myself,' Janice's mother busts in. 'I'm Veronica. This is Bradley, my fiancé. And who might you be?'

'I'm Peter, Janice's boyfriend.'

'No you're not,' says Janice, teeth so tight they creak. But her mother is cooing.

'So pleased to finally make your acquaintance. Why don't you join us?'

Her voice is louder than Janice's, and before she knows it, Peter is sharing the sangría, congratulating himself on the strawberries that have plopped into his glass, recommending the gambas al ajillo, and inserting the I'm-so-charming CD he played the night they first met. Janice's mother cannot help but be seduced.

Bradley notices Janice's displeasure. 'Why the long face, dear?' he asks, as if he's her stepfather already.

'Oh don't mind her,' says Janice's mother. 'She's always been moody.'

'Hey,' says Peter. 'I have my camera here. Would it bother anyone if I took your picture?'

'Not at all,' says Bradley.

'Get the hell away with your camera. I don't want to be in any more of your stupid movies,' says Janice.

Janice's mother is fixing her lipstick. 'Do I have anything in between my teeth?' she asks Tom.

'You look beautiful,' says Bradley, and Janice wants to be sick. Peter has already flicked open his digital camera and has pushed record. Janice has to do something. She pushes Peter with both hands.

'Did you hear me?' she says. 'Go.'

Peter stumbles backwards. Janice kicks his shins, and his camera catches flashes of her pointy toes, her sharp little heels, but remains steady in its resolve. 'Don't you have any boundaries?' she yells.

Peter shrugs, aims the camera at Janice's face. 'It's been great meeting you, Veronica, Bradley. But I think I'd better leave. The boys are waiting for me.' He walks backwards out the door, his camera still pointing at them. 'By the way, Janice, I got some great footage here. Thanks for your help.'

'Why did you have to send him away, Janice?' her mother asks. 'I liked him. He was dishy. Not like your other boyfriends: disasters, every one. Do you think he could film our wedding?'

All of a sudden Janice wants to pour the jug of sangría over her white dress. She has no scab to pick. 'He won't be filming your wedding, Mom. And neither will I, because I'm going to Barcelona.'

'You are? When did you decide that?'

Janice shrugs. She picks up her bag.

'Wait, you can't go! Who will be my bridesmaid?' her mother calls after her.

Janice walks out the door. She fumbles for a cigarette, the emergency break-up one stored in the secret compartment. Damn, no matches.

'Spare a quarter, Miss?' a homeless guy calls to her from the street corner.

'Sure,' she says, 'if you've got a light.'

And he does. She gives him a dollar. She takes a drag, emitting a dragon's nose of smoke.

'Feels good, huh?' says the homeless guy. 'Do you have a spare?'

'Sorry,' says Janice. 'This is my only one.' And then she leaves, walking south, trailing grey ribbons behind her.

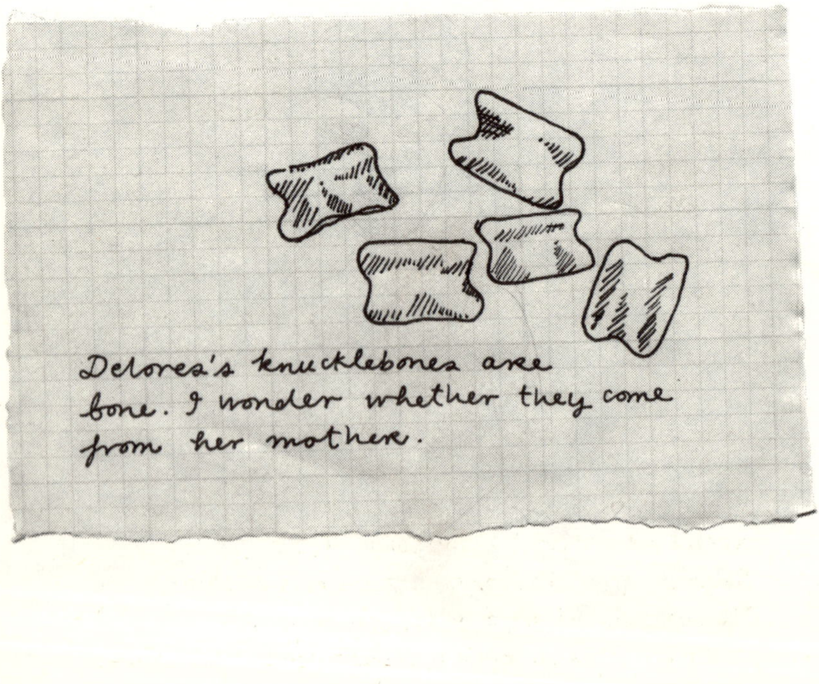
Delores's knucklebones are
bone. I wonder whether they come
from her mother.

Stepping on Cracks

Thrrrr-up, thrrr-up, thrrr-up go her fingers against the metal post. She's standing alone, stringy hair, corduroy skirt, scabby legs sprouting out of roman sandals. There's twenty more minutes of the lunch break to go, and her fingers are flicking out like the fan my uncle brought me back from Spain. Everyone else is in clusters, comparing friendship bracelets, playing hopscotch, sweeping pine needles into the corridors and bedrooms of imaginary houses. But she's standing alone, and so am I.

I didn't use to spend lunchtimes by myself. I used to have a friend, Stacey. But Stacey went to the Philippines with her family for the year, and now I have no one to play with. Mum tells me I have to say hello to people when I get to school. I whisper it. Hi. He-llo. 'No, Rebecca,' my mother says. 'You have to say, "Hello Monica, hello Kirsty, how are you?" '

I don't think so. Hello is enough. Hello is as hard as

having my teeth drilled, harder than when I ran the school cross-country, across paddocks, past dried cowpats and scrawny cabbage trees, abandoning my left sneaker in a muddy swamp because I was too tired to retrieve it. Hi, I whisper to the people who sit around me. They don't hear me; I can't catch their eye.

Mum knows about the girl whose fingers cascade against the post. Her family has moved next door to Mum's gossipy friend, who has collected an album of facts about her. The fact that her mother died of breast cancer. The fact that her father was knocked down by the truck he used to feed rubbish into, and now he can't work; now his words are muddied like green and red paint mixed together. The fact that she has a sister who's sixteen and had her stomach pumped of rum in the hospital, and that they are all looked after by her grandmother, who grows string beans up the fence that separates her from Mum's gossipy friend. Mum's gossipy friend picks the beans that grow through the slats, handing them back to the grandmother in exchange for facts. Sometimes she eats them, still warm from the sun.

'You should make friends with Dolores,' Mum tells me. 'She's just moved here; she doesn't know anybody. You could both do with a friend.'

Dolores. I turn the word over in my tongue like a boiled sweet. There's nobody else at school with that name. Dolores. It's Spanish, like my fan. Her mother was Spanish, before the cancer got her. I see her mother, whizzing around a cul-de-sac on a scooter, hair flying in the wind, her cleavage brown against her daisy-print dress, a dent in her arm where she was vaccinated against tuberculosis. I don't see her breastless. I don't see her dying.

Dolores. I finger a bag of raspberry drops in my pocket. The white paper feels soft like T-shirt cotton. Dolores hops from one tree stump to another in the schoolyard. I watch her, my bare feet plunged into the green grass, whispering he-llo. He-llo, Dolores.

'What are you staring at?' she says.

'Nothing. Do you want a lolly?'

'Thanks.' Dolores steps off the tree stump to reach for one. 'Do you want to play?'

'What do you do?'

'Leap across to every second stump; if you touch the ground, you turn to stone.'

Dolores leaps, wobbling as she lands. She turns and grins, her front tooth broken. 'Your turn,' she says.

I climb up onto the tree stump. I leap — I make it. I'm glad for my callused feet. I leap to the next stump. The next, the next. Dolores leaps after me. I leap again — I miss. The bark scrapes my shin. I scream, then swallow it. I breathe through the gaps between my teeth as the blood beads like droplets on get-well-card roses. Dolores looks pale.

'Come on, let's go to the sick bay,' she says. 'Which way is it?'

I point past the hopscotchers and the boys playing tag. I fix my eyes on a small hole in Dolores' T-shirt as I limp after her, the dribble of blood cooling my leg.

Dolores and I are friends. She has moved into the empty desk beside me, and when I get to school I say, 'Hi, Dolores,' easy as can be. We talk about what we saw on TV, and what we have in our sandwiches, and whether we have nicked enough five-cent pieces for K-bars from the kiosk. On wet days, when we can't go outside for lunch, we play knucklebones at the library. My knucklebones are aluminium and came in a small red bag. Dolores's are bone. I wonder whether they came from her mother. Dolores is much better at knucklebones than me. She never drops one; she can hold four in her fist while flicking the fifth from finger to finger. I wait my turn, combing the striped carpet with my nails. It takes my mind off picking my scab, something I know I shouldn't do, not in public anyway. But the scabs are ready beneath: they want to be flipped over like pancakes from the griddle, revealing the pink scars.

I invite Dolores to the movies on Friday night. *Return of the Jedi* is showing, and my favourite is Luke Skywalker. Dad is going to take us. We drive through the early evening, the sun in our eyes, showing up the squashed bugs and birdshit on the windscreen. He sits in the car listening to the radio as I run up the steps to Dolores' door. I knock quietly, then louder. There's a stagger-shuffle and the doorknob turns. The moustached man with a beer can in his hand must be her father.

'Whaddayouwan, sweedard?' he asks. 'I donhavany moneyfr Girl Guide bishcits, shodonask.'

'Is Dolores here?' I say, trying not to breathe in his smell.

'Uh. Oh. Dolores. Dolores!' he yells.

Dolores appears at the door.

'Bye, Dad,' she says, trying to sneak quickly past him.

'Dolores, Dolores honey. I loveyou, shweedheart. Darling, I loveyou. Don'tgo. Stay. Don'tgo. Bye-bye, shweedheart. Princess.' He covers Dolores in kisses: her hair, her cheeks, her eyes. She wriggles out, but he holds her wrist. 'Don'tgo, shweedheart. Stay withyour dad.' She breaks free and walks to the car, not looking back. But I do. Her father is sobbing, hoarse, tired-baby sounds, his beer can wedged between his head and the doorframe, squishing his eyebrow.

I'm glad to pull away from that house, where the concrete is painted green in the place of grass, and cigarette butts are mixed into the rock garden, some stuck to cactus prickles.

'Earth to Rebecca, have you done your homework yet?'

I didn't hear Dolores the first time. I was thinking of how I would want to wash my face with a hot flannel if my dad slobbered over me like her dad did. 'I'll do it on Sunday,' I say.

At the movies Dad buys us soft-serves and popcorn. Dolores pushes popcorn into her ice cream, then eats it. I copy her. The sweet ice cream seeps into the salty popcorn cracks. The end of the movie is the biggest shock. 'I'm your father,' wheezes Darth Vader, his face scarred like my shins when Luke takes off his black mask.

As the credits roll, I ask Dolores whether she wants to stay the night at my place. She nods.

'Will it be all right with your father?' Dad asks Dolores.

'He won't mind.'

'We'd better ring him to make sure.'

Dolores brushes popcorn off her lap as she stands, the seat snapping back like crocodile jaws. 'Okay,' she says.

Dolores and I have milky Milos and chocolate digestives at the kitchen table.

'Hello, am I speaking with Mr Rhodes?' asks Dad. The

receiver mumbles back at him. 'This is Rebecca's father. I was calling to see if Dolores can stay the night with Rebecca. We've got spare pyjamas and a new toothbru–'

Dad jerks the phone away from his ear. The receiver is hacking now, choking on bad words and spittle flying down the wire.

'Mr Rhodes, this is quite unnecessary. In the state you're in, I think it would be better–'

Hmmmmmmmmm.

My father is flushed. 'Well,' he says. 'Well.' He pushes his glasses back up his nose, he smoothes back strands of displaced hair. 'Rebecca, go and find Dolores a pair of your pyjamas. I'll set up the trundle bed.'

Dolores and I whisper ourselves to sleep. We sing songs under our breath, we swap favourite colours. 'You're my best friend,' I tell her at midnight, the time you're allowed to say anything you like. 'I've only had one best friend before. You can keep my pyjamas if you like.'

'Thanks,' she says.

When I wake up at 4am to go to the toilet, Dolores is staring up at the plaster roses on the ceiling.

'Dolores?' I say.

She flicks her eyes shut.

Dolores has made a new friend, Theresa. Her father is the local butcher, and she shares her string of cheerios with us at lunchtime. Theresa plays knucklebones with us when it rains, and hopscotch on sunny days. I get to school early so I can practise. I want to be better than Theresa; I'm sick of her always winning. Even though we all hang out at lunchtime, she has only shown Dolores the bruise her dad gave her when she tripped over her new bicycle and spilled the pigs' scrap bucket.

My bicycle is pretty rusty but it's not as bad as Dolores's. She has my mother's gossipy friend's old bicycle, stiffened by years in the garage, the seat pushed down so that her legs can reach the pedals. We are biking to the swimming pool, our towels stuffed into our front baskets, our swimming togs on underneath our school clothes. I love the fish-scale feel of the nylon on my skin, the way my T-shirt slides across it. The only problem is when I want to pee. Then I have to undress in the changing-room toilets, my shorts soaking up chlorinated water on the concrete floor. We're going to lie our towels out across the dry grass and sunbathe, the smell of coconut oil around us. When we're too hot, we'll either dive into the pool or pick our way across the bodies and prickles and buy something to eat with the $2 note I have tucked down my front.

Dolores and Theresa are whispering. I sit up, trying to join in, but they have curtained themselves off with their long hair. I lie on my pink towel, wondering whether I should get a Jelly-Tip or maybe salt and vinegar chips and a Coke. Dolores is showing Theresa something. It looks like a burn on the inside of her arm. They whisper some more. My eyes sting. I jump up and dive into the pool, where my tears can mix with the water, along with the spit and pee and ice-block dribble. You can't splash and do underwater handstands by yourself, so I swim a length, and then another, sliding up and down the black line like an abacus bead. If I make sixteen lengths on school swimming day I will get a gold sticker to go on my certificate.

When I touch the end of the pool at length number eight, Theresa and Dolores are parting their legs on the bottom of the pool and taking turns to dive between them.

'My turn, my turn!' I yell. I dive down and swim through Dolores's legs, kicking strongly as I go.

She is grimacing when I come up. 'You kicked me in the privates,' she says.

Theresa glares at me, hand on Dolores's shoulder.

We walk our bicycles home, togs still wet under our clothes, hair drying in clumps. The sun is low; there's the smell of sausages and steak frying in people's back yards. I pick my way around the welts in the pavement.

'Step on a crack, break your mother's back,' I say to Dolores.

'Your mother's,' she says.

How could have I forgotten? I want the cracks to gape.

'You're so insensitive, Rebecca,' says Theresa.

Dolores smiles, hooking her arm through Theresa's elbow, straightening the wobble in her bicycle. 'It's great to finally have a best friend. You're a friend, Rebecca, but not like Theresa.'

I slow, slow, slow down. Theresa didn't even want to be Dolores's friend until I was friends with her. It was me: I took the first step, I said hello. Hello Delores, how are you? I showed her which part of the school guinea pig to press to make his penis pop out. I didn't say anything when she wrote her name on my eraser.

I bite my lip, gripping my handlebars so the metal digs into my skin. I stomp on every crack because this is all Mum's fault; I should have waited for Stacey to come back from the Philippines.

Dolores and Theresa don't notice when I turn down the

shortcut. I duck under the iron barriers, then climb back on my bicycle. I experiment with no hands, grabbing hold of the brakes when Dolores calls my name. But when I turn, she isn't waiting for me. Perhaps I never heard her voice in the first place.

"Why you not listen to classical? You frighten my pigeons."

PERFECT

The porridge glunks to the highchair where Sam spilt it this morning. There is a piece of banana on the bench, trawled by sluggish flies. Martha huffs at the fringes of our house, clipping her hedge, wanting to be asked inside for a brandy that I don't have. I refuse to invite her outdated parenting advice. Sam sleeps. This is my time. Should I clean up? Or should I sit down with a cup of tea and a magazine?

Too late: there he cries, and no amount of patting will post him back into the box of sleep. He is up, imploring me. What does he want? Words start with firm consonants and trail away, a shooting star of meaning to wish upon. I press him to me, his tears wetting my neck. I open the fridge, saying *shhhh, shhhh* — shit. There is no milk. There are only condiment jars, lids scabbed shut, and a flaccid spring onion. I fill a sippy cup with water, and give Sam a biscuit. He quietens, pulping it in his mouth and on his chin. I check his nappy (only a little wet), then heft him out the door into his buggy.

The sky is curdled, a whey of cloud floating above our heads. Drizzle spritzes our cheeks so I seal the buggy in plastic. Sam pushes his hands and feet against it. We walk past the state houses, and the boy who sings from his kitchen window stops. He is too young to not be in school. I smile at him, wanting him to keep singing, but I hear the clunk of dishes instead.

Tufts of fennel fray the footpath, and I side-step a mound of regurgitated cat food. We walk past the abandoned fifties strip mall, past the burnt-out Chinese takeaway, past the empty gun shop, shelves raided for a forgotten heist. I imagine the shop I would open there. It would have rose-patterned teacups and 1960s dresses. I would make cushion covers while Sam pushed his train around a wooden track. But would anyone around here want to buy that sort of thing?

I cross the road and the neighbourhood improves. The houses are freshly painted. Their verandas are cabled in wisteria, hedges clipped in the shape of French holidays.

Her house is perfect. Pale green, Georgian, blue-grey shuttered windows. Her gold Peugeot is not parked in the drive today, so I peek through the bevelled glass door at the vase of irises on her hall table. Irises run parallel to the picket fence. Everything glimmers; I have seen her polishing. I tiptoe around the corner of the house to see her son's felt mobile above his cot; I glimpse the expensive linen in the guest room.

She appears the same age as me, and sometimes she is wrestling her same-age-as-Sam son into the car as I pass. Her blonde curls are French-twisted, no tendrils escaping, even when she pushes her hand-mower along her rectangle of grass. My hair is damaged, half blonde, half brown, the roots a statement of neglect rather than fashion. I knot my hair around itself and its fibres mesh so I do not need a tie. Her body is lean and wiry, clothed in clean white T-shirts and crisp upturned jeans. She irons. Her legs are waxed and brown. I look down at my banana-stained op-shop dress, the brocaded roses unravelling. I look down at my scuffed shoes, my white unshaven legs, scaly patches revealing my lack of moisturiser. I don't think we can be friends.

I pick up speed. Sam demands Coke cans from the gutter. He flails his arms, thumps his feet. He rips at the plastic cover and the Velcro releases with the sound of a cleared throat. The plastic gets caught in the wheels. 'Almost there,' I say. 'Calm down.' Those words would inflame me.

The dairy step is high so I leave the buggy outside. Sam squashes his fingers into the strawberry punnets and I yank him away. The woman behind the counter glares. I select my milk and place my hank of bananas on the scales, and she registers the total. I chatter about the weather but she is busy watching the surveillance video. She places a receipt in my palm, and it buckles, coins sliding onto the counter. Her children play snakes with licorice straps. I wonder if they will be returned to the box for sale.

Sam pushes his buggy down the footpath, veering off the kerb. I pick him up and wipe the leaves off his bottom. By the time we get back to the Georgian house she is in the driveway, taking her blonde boy out of his carseat. Her stomach is sticking out where once it was flat. Is she pregnant? I cast a backward glance. Yes, she is. I feel an ache. I resent that there will be no full brothers or sisters for Sam.

I see traces of Matt at his mother's place. She is an enthusiastic grandmother; not one I would choose. She babysits so I can revisit my old life. The bars are still there. They host bands and serve beer to my friends, who look young in the dim light. When Sam stays with her, Matt stops by. She thinks I don't recognise the stench of his sneakers she's pushed under the sofa, their toes peeking out from under the frill. Sam returns in new clean clothes, clutching educational toys, smelling of the disinfectant she liberally applies. And also, faintly, of Matt's cigarettes.

Sam is grizzling, an insistent drone. Shhh, I say. But it is too late, there is Martha, hosing the bread she has spread across her lawn. The pigeons shuffle on my rooftop, waiting for her to turn off the tap.

'What a beautiful baby,' she sing-songs, her voice clotted with the old country. 'You are so beautiful, a beautiful boy! Look, I have a lollipop for you.' She keeps her pockets loaded.

'He doesn't need a lollipop,' I say, imagining the roots of his teeth going brown. But it's too late now.

'Unwrap this for me, Anna. My hands, they cannot do it.'

I tear it open with my teeth, wishing I had got my key out of my bag earlier so we could have avoided this. Sam giggles as he slurps the sweet.

'You have a clever skull — look at his skull, such a clever shape!'

I wonder whether she is a phrenologist.

'But why are you sad, Sam? It is because he is cold. Why did you not put him in a hat? And he needs a raincoat.'

'He's fine.'

'You don't look like your mother; are you like your father? But I don't know what your father looks like. Who does Sam look like, Anna?'

'He looks like Sam.'

'Well, Sam, you come and visit me. Come and visit your Aunty Martha. I will teach you how to whistle.'

I smile and push him inside. I smile as I shut the door in her face. I pry the sticky sweet from Sam's hand and then return it to him when his cries are too loud. I slosh some milk into a small pot on the stove to heat. Sam sits at my feet, dribbling red sugar, and pulls the pots out of the cupboard. Whoowop-whooowop-whooowop, drum the spinning lids. The noise is loud enough to lift the carpet of pigeons, and they swoop around in formation, shedding feathers, before resettling on the shit-corroded roof.

'Mil-, mil-,' Sam says to the pot on the stove.

'It's coming, patience.' I open his bottle and pour the milk in, screwing the lid tight. He grabs it and sucks it down.

Every Friday I walk Sam to crèche. I pass the boy, who hasn't yet begun to sing. I pass my shop, the sunlight dancing off the dust. I pass the Georgian house just after eight and, if I am lucky, she is kissing her husband goodbye from her red doorstep. At 3pm I pick Sam up, splotched with paint and snot. The teachers unnerve me: they mention his hearing, his tendency to trip, his sensitivity. Is everything all right at home?

I am running late today, but so is she. Her back presses against the closed door; her son smears his face on the glass. Her husband flaps across the road in his trenchcoat, mowing his chin with a battery-powered razor. There is a sign newly stapled to the picket fence: *For Sale*. There will be an open home on Sunday.

When I return, Martha is unloading boxes of bread from her car. She arranges them in order of staleness along the wall of her garage.

'Anna, hello, where is Sam? He has not gone to crèche, has he?'

'Yes,' I say. We have the same conversation each week.

'But he is too young! He needs to be with his mother. He also needs his father — when is his father coming home?'

'He's not.' I wonder where her husband and children are. If she has any.

'And Anna,' she calls after me as I open my door, as I close it behind me. 'He will get sick. It can happen so quickly. They are well, and then they are . . . ' She pauses for breath, 'gone.'

I scramble three eggs on Sunday: one for me, one for Sam, one for my old life of hangover brunches and sleep-ins till midday. These days I rise at 6.30. I serve Sam's egg with toast soldiers. He grabs a handful. The egg slops down his front. I should change him before we leave the house, disguised as potential home-buyers.

There are no clean clothes so I scrape the egg off Sam's T-shirt. I wipe his nose; I pull a hat down over his ears. I wrench a jersey over his head and add a jacket.

The real estate agent wears a pinstriped suit. The plates on his BMW are personalised SELALL.

'Do you mind parking the buggy around the side? It's disrupting the indoor-outdoor flow.' He sniffs at our scuffed shoes, which we kick off at the door, clearing his throat when I take three of the branded chocolates on offer.

The irises on the hall table are repeated on embroidered cushions and a large oil painting. Her son's toys are wooden. Their bed is massive, the eiderdown ripe. On the walls are their black and white wedding photos. She is laughing, head thrown back, his lips at the nape of her neck. They are on the beach, his trousers rolled, her dress hitched up. The sea laps their ankles. Their appliances gleam. Their iris-coloured sofa is unmarked by felt-tip pens. Their books are coffee-table sized. They look out on a green valley.

'Thanks,' I call brightly, as I carry Sam out the door. The real estate agent straightens his tie in the mirror. We are the river silt to be washed away from the gold.

I am making lunch when I hear the door opening. I realise that the knock was not from the song on the radio Sam and I had been dancing to.

What is *she* doing here? Did the real estate agent say something? Has she noticed me spying?

'Something's burning.' She puts her son down, pointing behind me. Smoke puffs from the grill. I pull the fish fingers out, dousing them with water in the sink. I look up; she is still there.

'Sorry to bother you. It's your neighbour — she's taken a fall down the steps. I heard her calling when we were going for a walk. Can you help me lift her into the house?'

Uncharitable thoughts flood my mind. If Martha's hurt herself she won't be able to feed the pigeons. This is her way of summoning Sam and me. This will get her out of our hair for a while. But if I fell, who would help me? 'Sure,' I say.

I lift Sam onto my hip and follow her along the pathway that joins our places. Martha is slumped on the steps, looking pale, her legs stretched out in front of her.

'There you are, Anna. Didn't you hear me? I have sprained my ankle; I cannot stand up on it.' She gestures at the left one. It is puffy and red, but so is the right. 'I was taking this roll of grass down and I slipped. I am too old for this.' She waves at the roulade of green and an upturned wheelbarrow.

'I'm sorry. I had my music up.'

'Your music is always too loud, Anna. Loud and yelling. Why you not listen to classical? You frighten my pigeons. And Sam will go deaf.'

'He'll be fine,' I say through gritted teeth, crouching so that she can lean her weight on my shoulder.

'Lucky this beautiful young lady was passing. But she cannot lift me with a belly like that. What is your name?'

'Xanthe.' She grabs Sam's hand as he tries to make a break for the road.

Martha hops beside me to the door. I open it and we stagger, three-legged, towards her armchair. When we arrive she collapses into it. 'Pass me my ottoman,' she says. I push it towards her. It is covered in zebra skin, and I wonder if it is real. She has told me that after the revolution, she lived in South Africa. 'Help me,' she says. I lift her foot onto the ottoman and loosen her shoelaces, looking up at the cutlassed horsemen that rear on her wall. 'Thank you, and now, please, a brandy — is good for health.' She waves at the liquor cabinet against the wall.

'I'll get it,' says Xanthe. The boys grab at the copper ashtray, the African spear. Xanthe confiscates them. She pulls the crystal stopper out of the decanter and she dispenses an expert two fingers. She must practise on her husband's gins.

'You, have one too. Good for baby.' Martha gulps hers. Sam clears the coffee table of magazines.

'Can I get you an ice-pack?' Xanthe asks.

'A what?'

Xanthe rummages through the freezer, returning with a packet of frozen peas. 'We'll use these instead.'

'You are having a drink with me?'

Xanthe shakes her head while rubbing her stomach. 'What will you eat with your peas tonight? Shall I get some chops out as well?'

'But my lawn. How will I fix it now? The pigeons have eaten my grass. It's like concentration camp. If only there were strong men around here.' She looks at me as if it is my failing alone.

'Don't worry. We'll sort it out,' Xanthe offers, refilling Martha's glass.

The lawn roll is heavy, and I lift it into the wheelbarrow by myself while Xanthe entertains the children. 'I'll help you lay it,' she offers. I wobble it down the path, using my weight as a counter-balance. I tip it out where I think it should begin. We kneel, side by side, as if at church.

We push the roll and the grass creaks, reluctant to loosen its grip on the roots above. We roll until we have covered all but a sliver of dirt. The boys pull the flowers off Martha's pansies. Their golden heads dazzle in the sunlight. Xanthe sits on the new lawn, her face red from the effort. Her son throws himself across her lap, his feet and arms reaching out either side. Sam tries to do roly-polies. I collapse beside Xanthe.

She slumps back, staring up at the sky. 'Ow!' she says. 'I shouldn't lie like this; the baby squashes my arteries.' She sits up again. 'I see you out walking,' she says. 'You always wear such interesting clothes.'

'Thanks.' I wonder if she means it as a compliment. 'I want to open a shop in that place down the road, sell re-engineered dresses and retro china.'

'You should; I love little shops. Would you serve coffee as well? I'd be your best customer. I mean, I would be if we weren't moving away.'

'You are? Where are you going?'

'The Hawke's Bay. Back in with my parents — can you believe it? I need all the help I can get with another one due.'

'I couldn't live with my parents. Has your husband got a job there?' I ask.

'My dad keeps on offering Greg a job at his bank. He doesn't understand why Greg thinks it's a come-down. You work in London, you work in Wellington; it's hard to go back to the provinces. Anyway, he's got the apartment to live in while he finds himself something more suitable.'

'You have an apartment? How glamorous.'

'Just one of those inner-city cubes. Wouldn't want

to live there myself — it's an investment property. The tenant, on the other hand: *she's* glamorous.'

'How great would that be, living in the city.' I miss the city; I thought Sam needed a backyard.

'Greg seems to be having trouble evicting her. She's a girl from his work; he's been suggesting keeping her on as a flatmate. He says that way we won't have to find a new tenant when he moves north. I really don't like that idea.'

'Do you think they're . . . ?'

'No, no. Greg tells me the pregnancy hormones are making me paranoid. I just feel so huge and unattractive. Greg says I'm sexier this way, but he's such a liar.'

'You're glowing,' I say, remembering how puffy I was.

'Am I?' She puts her hand to her cheek.

'My boyfriend left me when I was pregnant.'

'Really? What a bastard. Greg would never leave me. She's just a tenant. She's half his age. Long black hair, that vampy look.'

'We weren't really suited to each other anyway. I got pregnant the second time I slept with him. He cried every night for a week after I told him. It's the worst time to break up, before you give birth. I don't think I've ever felt so–'

'Marvellous!' There is Martha, leaning on a moss-covered pillar. She stretches out her free hand to pinch Sam's cheek but he shrinks away from her. 'Thank you, ladies.'

'Shouldn't your foot be elevated?' I snap.

'Get off the grass, Anna, you are squashing it.'

I offer Xanthe my hand, and she is as heavy as the lawn roll. She stands astride the blades, uncrinkling at her ankles like freshly hatched butterfly wings. The smell of summer flits around us.

'It's so green,' I say, fighting the urge to fall forward, burying my face in it.

'You'd never guess it was bare earth a moment ago,' says Xanthe, tucking a strand back into her French twist, rubbing her belly. 'All covered up so neatly.'

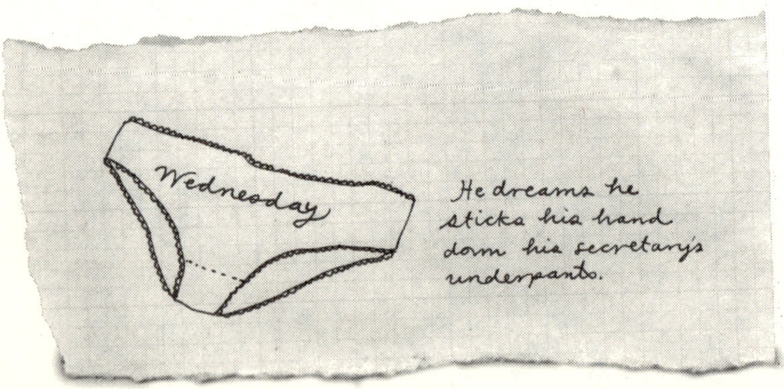
Wednesday
He dreams he
sticks his hand
down his secretary's
underpants.

STING *Ray*

Natasha floats in the cove, the silk sea sliding across the earth's hips. She ebbs, hemmed in by rocks.

Martin is at the bach. He sleeps, the sour milk smell of too much pinot clouding above him.
The borer hum in the walls. The fridge sings, the cistern whispers. He has not awoken to the sock tongue.
He dreams of old-fashioned trading boards, numbers scrambling beneath his fingers. He dreams he is caught in a shower of zeroes and twos. He dreams he sticks his hand down his secretary's underpants. They are white, and they say *Wednesday*.

Natasha floats. She imagines the Pacific as the bottom lip, the Mediterranean as the top. She is in the seam between. Her daughter waves at her from Costa Brava, and Natasha waves back. The dreadlocks have been shorn from Emily's head and she has taken the bolt of metal out of her tongue. She is no longer with Sophie but lies on a striped towel with Jaume, a boy she met in Barcelona. Jaume and Emily shake the sand from their golden skin. They swim towards her; they will join Martin and Natasha on the deck for brioches and coffee. They will discuss buying real estate together and Emily will have forgiven Natasha for what she said about Sophie because it was just a silly phase.

The brioches have risen enough to be put in the oven, but Natasha doesn't want to return to shore. The sea is smooth enough for clouds to be screen-printed on it. It holds her more gently than Martin does, massaging the knots from her shoulders.

She sees a black shape approach her. A diver. She will bring her snorkel and mask down next time.

No. What looks like a man, wetsuited, with his arms outspread, is a stingray. Natasha scrambles onto the nearest rock, barnacles cutting into her instep, her breath frayed, her floaty brain belly-flopped. The stingray circles, its tail a braid. What does it want from her? She is not tasty, her nutrients are long-since leached. *Go away*, she implores.

And it does, but Natasha can't float any more.

Martin is hammering a piece of trellis to the end of the deck. Each blow cracks his head in two, and the brioches churn, but he is the penitent kind. He planted bougainvillea on their last holiday and it has bolted, gangling shoots willy-nilly. He will secure them with Natasha's laddered tights, chopped into strips.

Natasha licks her finger and scans the bench for crumbs. She finds a nugget of white chocolate. She takes her scrapbooking box off the top of the singing fridge.

She selects a piece of citrus paper to offset the grapefruit picture. The photograph is yellowed. Emily must be about nine. Her leg is slung over the fence Martin built, and she bites into the half-peeled grapefruit. Behind her rises the tree, studded with happy faces. Although the grapefruit are tart and swaddled in pith, Emily enjoys hers, her face sweet and open. After the photograph, Emily will leap off the fence and graze her knee. Natasha will carry her inside and pick the gravel from the wound. Natasha can still feel Emily's soft, sunbaked hair, and remember the smell of peel.

Natasha cuts a length of ribbon to bow above the photograph. She snips a rectangle of double-sided tape. She uses silver pen for the black paper. *Emily eating the sun.* She has asked Customs to inform her if Emily returns. She has reported Emily missing to both the police and Foreign Affairs. The young man at the call centre suggested that Emily might be having time out, she probably wasn't dead. He hadn't called his mum for nine months. Natasha told him to do so, quelling her horror at the thought.

Natasha has sent emails apologising, but Emily never replies. The last email bounced back from the mail administrator. Emily has floated off to find a better family, one that she has chosen. *I wasn't thinking when I said it*, wrote Natasha.

'Goddamnit!' yells Martin. The hammer has slipped. She goes to the freezer for the ice.

Natasha sips her pinot in the night violet. She toe-combs the sand, probing for a cooler place.

Martin is sitting in his chair. It faces north, as it does at home. He has finished his air-freighted *Wall Street*

Journal and now reads *Harper's*, other people's tragedies finely wrought. They do not talk about their own. Martin agrees with the call-centre boy. He skipped off around the world when he was twenty-one, not returning for five years after only six letters to his mother. He brought his first million home with him.

But there have been no letters, thinks Natasha. She will have this glass of wine, and Martin will finish the bottle. He has brought a few cases. Natasha cannot tell where one bottle ends and the next begins. She looks at the sky.

Star light, star bright, first star I see tonight . . .

The wish is single and constant. When she was younger she had a plethora. *Rich husband, career as ceramic artist, house by the sea, beautiful baby . . .* Most of them were granted. It was just a matter of waiting.

Natasha slips off her dress and walks into the sea in her underpants. It is a sequined, patent-leather slick, still warm but cooling beneath the surface.

She floats. Crabs scuttle beneath her. Wherever she moves, the sea glows. Natasha's eyes are closed; she is unaware of the phosphorescence.

She imagines Emily on the Costa Brava, her hair still dreaded. One arm rests on Sophie's bare thigh, the other one waves at Natasha. Natasha waves back. *Swim towards me,* she thinks. *We'll have a pinot on the shore.* But Emily and Sophie stand and pull jeans up over their sandy bottoms. They walk towards the road and disappear into the traffic.

Natasha's head hits something. She opens her eyes, suddenly aware of her illumination in the dark. She jumps onto the familiar barnacled rock.

STINGRAY

There is a silvery outline of a man, his arms and legs outstretched in a star.

'Hello?' Natasha calls.

The man floats by, his eyes closed. Where has he come from? He wears draw-string shorts that flare like wings. The moon glints on his chin. She touches him with her toe.

He starts, sinking below and then rising. A milky way surrounds him. She slides off the rock to hide her nakedness.

'Hello,' she says.

'Hello,' he says. 'You frightened me.'

'Sorry. Who are you?'

'I'm from there,' he says, pointing beyond the cove. 'Who are you?'

'I'm Natasha. I'm from here.' She looks at her bach, which seems distant.

The man reaches out and touches her. 'You're glowing,' he says. 'It's the algae.'

Natasha has a can of pepper spray for strange men in the street. Not here. The man swirls algae around one breast and then the other. He swims closer and puts his mouth at her nipple. Natasha lets him suck it to the back of his throat. She breastfed Emily until she was two. He tugs her further into the sea, then pulls away.

Natasha dives under the water. He dives down with her. *You are beautiful*, he writes, as if his finger were a sparkler. Natasha grimaces; it is no longer true. She hears Martin call for someone else in his sleep. But when she looks down, silver shimmers around her. The man takes her hand. *Shall we dance?*

At first Natasha stumbles, sure she is missing the air,

but then they twirl and dip, foxtrot and pirouette. *Come*, spells the man. They are swimming into the ballroom of wrecked ship, the chandelier still slung from the ceiling. The cellos spring up from their slumber, they swoon to their steps, bows strung with seaweed.

'Natasha!' she hears Martin calling, but he is muffled and distant. 'Natasha!' he calls again, and his voice is full of longing.

Natasha presses herself into the man, kissing his neck, his collarbone, his lips. His black wings embrace her. Something sharp presses into her ankle. She jerks away, but she is caught. A braid spirals around her body.

She spins to unwind it; she yanks its hook from her flesh. The cellos play a polka, seaweed snapping with the strain. Natasha escapes through the porthole. The man follows her. *Jaume*, he spells.

Where is Emily? Natasha writes, but he has disappeared.

'We don't have any ice left,' says Martin, crouching beside her. She is sitting on his chair, a towel between her and its leather skin. 'But I think a bucket of hot water is better for these things.'

Natasha reaches out her hand to touch Martin's hair. It is wet, and he wears his towelling robe.

'Is it safe to swim drunk?' she asks.

'I had no choice,' says Martin. 'Did you see it glow?'

Natasha nods. 'Algae,' she says.

'Oh?' says Martin. He is the one who usually wins at Trivial Pursuit. He stands to fill the bucket. Natasha tries to stand as well but her ankle gives way. He helps her back into the chair. 'I was thinking we should have a holiday. Not just at the bach — somewhere overseas. I need to stop dreaming about work.'

'Yes,' says Natasha.

'What about the Mediterranean?' he calls out over the roar of the tap.

Costa Brava, spells Natasha.

Josh remembers the
elephant from the
Wellington Zoo, ears
blown back, a
load of
sugar-hyped
kids on
its back.

SWEDEN

The cable grommet is not a success. It is beautiful — a computer cord stem threaded through a fuchsia blossom eyelet to emerge as a stamen — but the petals have sharp edges. Each time Josh jiggles his leg under his desk he snags his trousers. He fears he may roll his chair forward too quickly and slice his artery lengthwise. Josh's products often have menace within them, only revealed after the prototype phase.

Lately, he has been feeling angry for no good reason. He wonders whether his subconscious is surfacing. Mathilde has suggested that he take up boxing at the gym, but the appointments Josh makes with his personal trainer come and go, and he is unable to tear himself from his CAD drawing or his important client meeting.

Mathilde says he is a workaholic, but that is how they got together in the first place. An all-nighter in preparation for a big pitch, 3am, no one else in the studio. They did it on the drafting table, on the stack of photocopy paper, on the boardroom table, and then he went around with Spray n'Wipe and paper towels to clean up the mess, while Mathilde giggled, cajoling him to do it one more time. Even then work took precedence. No, he said, I *have* to finish this presentation. It's almost there, just another hour. Mathilde shrugged and shut down her computer. I'll leave you to it, she said.

And she has. She has quit Zusters & Mensch, but not before designing a delightful package for the baby T-shirts she hand-embroiders in the sunroom overlooking the sea. Josh suspects she wants a baby but he has never raised the issue with her. Nor has he sat much in the sunroom, as he is at work during daylight hours, and when he is not at work he is researching design stores or in his at-home studio.

The phone rings as he is perfecting the curve of his shelf bracket. It is Mathilde. He thinks about ignoring it, but she has been accusing him of having an affair.

'We got another wedding invite,' she says, by way of hello. Her vowels have been distorted by five years in New Zealand, and it compromises the sexiness of her French accent.

'Who from this time?' he asks.

'Thea and Violet,' she says.

'Oh, a lesbian wedding,' he says. He finds the idea rather exciting.

'Don't be like that. It's at a vineyard. And I know you're going to try and back out, because you're too busy, but listen, Thea's family are very rich, and they are always redecorating, so you may wish to introduce yourself and your funny little things.'

'I wouldn't miss two dykes getting hitched.'

SWEDEN

'Salaud. When are you coming home?'

Josh looks at the time on the computer. 8.13pm. 'In half an hour, chéri. Early.'

'Whatever.' She hangs up on him. She does that a lot these days. She wants him to come home earlier, but that just makes him dig his toes in. Does Mathilde expect a proposal from him? It is true that they have been attending a lot of weddings lately and Mathilde cries at every single one. Josh pretends not to notice.

On the way home he stops at the dairy to buy a bunch of lilies and a bottle of wine. As he walks down the chipped steps, the pizza delivery boys survey his BMW.

'Don't you have work to do? I think I can hear a Hawaiian coming through,' he says. He bares his incisors and two of the three clear off.

'Cool car,' says the bravest of the three. 'Z4, huh? Six cylinder, four valve. You must be a big man. How many seconds to a hundred k?'

Josh grunts. 'Dunno. I just appreciate good design.'

'So do I, man. So do I. Can I have a ride?'

Josh appraises the boy. Lanky, designer jeans hanging off his pointy hips, a constellation of pimples at his brow. Still, good bone structure and a thick head of black hair. The boy kicks a can and then raises his long eyelashes to Josh's face, slowly, seductively.

'I don't think so,' Josh says. He hops in the car and accelerates out of the park. Four seconds to fifty k. The boy shrinks in his rear-view mirror.

Mathilde is in front of the television when he arrives. Outside the stars skid off the wave tops and the moon dribbles silver to the shore. Mathilde is watching *The Bachelorette.* The contenders line up in their prom dresses and show their newly capped teeth to the arsehole who gets to choose. His qualifications? Money: made from bin-liners or postal labels. Why they would want to marry such a dullard for a million bucks is beyond him. Josh takes the vase out of the alcove and chucks the last lot of lilies into the bin. He snips the pollen off the new bunch so they won't stain the white wall. Mathilde looks up as he arranges the stalks and returns them to their place.

'More white lilies? Don't you know that red is the colour of passion? But then again, white suits you.'

'Hi, darling, how was work today?'

She doesn't answer. The bachelorettes are in their swimsuits, leaping into an infinity pool. He opens the freezer, quelling the voice that says Mathilde should cook him dinner. She refuses to cook for someone who isn't going to be there to eat with her.

'But you are French,' he has argued. 'You eat late.'

'I am from Brittany,' she replies. 'I do not eat at nine or ten or whenever it is you decide to come home.'

Ting, goes the microwave, and Josh opens the door, which seamlessly melds into the wall, and removes the plastic wrap. Although it says chicken fricassée with gratinéed sweet potatoes and julienned French beans, it could be anything.

'Fuck,' he says as he burns the roof of his mouth. He plops down on the sofa next to Mathilde. She puts her hand under his bum. For a moment he thinks everything is okay, then she pulls out the remote that he is sitting on, and turns up the volume.

'I don't want to hear you swallowing,' she says.

Josh sighs. He looks at the predictably breathtaking view, and then at his feature wall, the vase recessed within it. The wallpaper is three-dimensional and modular, each square rising in meringue peaks. Thanks to careful lighting, the tones graduate to eggshell. This piece won him awards and a feature article in *Vogue Living*, looking relaxed and chic in his expensive shirt, Mathilde an exotic blur in the kitchen, making coffee and crêpes or some other definitively-French-and-only-for-the-photo-shoot fancy. The magazine sits on their coffee table, plastic protecting its year-old cover. He revisits it to reassure himself that he *has* been a success.

Because you're worth it, the television says to the girls who shampoo. But are they? What have they done except be born in the right place at the right time? And is he still worth it? He hasn't made anything breathtaking since the wallpaper, and there are young designers willing to work longer hours and take more risks. The young designers don't have to come home by nine. They don't have girlfriends at all.

He bends down to find it but it is not there.

'Mathilde, what have you done with my magazine?'

'I put it away. I need the space for my sewing kit.'

'Where is it?' he asks, trying to remain calm.

'I don't know. Maybe the study? Or perhaps the basement?'

Josh slaps his meal down on the floor and stomps off to the study. It is on the desk, tossed so that the cover has turned back on itself. Across the work bench are Mathilde's latest T-shirts, each image lovingly stitched. He fingers the gnome, the swan. He fingers the ballerina and the puppy dog. He hopes she is being ironic.

He smoothes the cover (he'll have to press it beneath his design books) and turns to page sixty-three, where his feature begins. Everything is in harmony with his mental image of his life. The wall is without the nicks and dents it has acquired, without the sausage-dog tooth punctures from when Violet and Thea came to stay. It calms him, as would a prayer. He flicks a few pages over. Funnily enough, Violet and Thea made it into the same magazine. But they are the contrast piece, their apartment cluttered and filled with found ephemera, none of it produced after 1962. All of their furniture is half-sanded and hand-painted, and their infernal dog wears a crocheted rose on his collar.

Violet and Thea met on the set of a play, where Thea was the costume designer and Violet was the set designer. Now they are an unstoppable duo, creating lavish and uncompromising stage shows that disturb, and reveal what it truly means to be human. Costumes layer the backs of chairs, and torn-out photos from magazines collage their walls. In their fruit bowl there is pineapple, quince, plum, durian and a chewed tennis ball. Josh feels claustrophobic even contemplating the picture. He carries Sweden inside him, the glacial peninsula drifting around his organs.

'I am going to bed,' Mathilde calls. Josh wonders whether he should follow her to their white room and slide along her body, between the Egyptian cotton sheets. Make peace. But he is tired, and desire requires effort. He turns on the computer, opens up a prototype that he has saved for such occasions. When his wrist hurts, he climbs onto his Le Corbusier recliner and goes to sleep.

The wedding is a cacophony of light and colour, and Josh uses his black turtleneck and pants as a force-field against excess. Mathilde is at home in magenta, and she has swiped a glass of champagne from a jester, has wiggled her hips along a line of flaring trumpets. They have passed through a tunnel of scarlet silk and are now in a saffron marquee, chandeliers encrusting the ceiling with a thousand crystal lenses. In the middle is a pond studded with lotus blossoms and goldfish. The lily pads have been engineered to hold champagne flutes, but some of them have already toppled into the water.

Everybody is so outrageous. There are transvestites who are at least seven foot tall in their wigs. Feathers sprout from their bums, tickling Josh's face when they pass. Mathilde is kissing her colleagues from the set design world she inhabited before she joined Zusters & Mensch. 'Darling, darling,' he can hear all around her. 'Mwah, mwah, mwah. But why did you leave us? Your ice sculptures were out of this world . . . '

' . . . Yes, and remember when they all started to melt in the middle of a show and the actor slipped on the slick and broke his leg?'

'No, it was his little finger.'

' . . . Is that why you left, darling? You couldn't get over the guilt?'

' . . . Or maybe you were going to be sued?'

'Merde, he wasn't using that finger anyway. It was too far stuck up his arse.'

Mathilde is in her element, her face radiant, her French accent pronounced. She is that mercurial, foul-mouthed creature who first blew into the studio, not the languid needlepoint freak he finds himself living with. But then again, he is hardly ever there — what does he know what she's like?

The canapés are delicious: little duck and pastry explosions, oysters in shot glasses, tomatillo salsas that electrify the tongue. It is funny that Violet and Thea are having a wedding breakfast before the ceremony, but they like to challenge assumptions.

Suddenly there is a fanfare. The trumpets and saxophones scream: Dixieland meets psychedelia. The silk door bulges. Violet and Thea sit on a real elephant, underneath a canopy of scarlet. Where the hell did they get that? Josh remembers the elephant from the Wellington Zoo, ears blown back in the wind, a load of sugar-hyped kids on its back. When it died they didn't replace it.

Violet and Thea shower rose petals on the guests. When they reach the middle of the marquee Violet lifts a horn to her lips and toots. 'Follow us,' she cries.

The wedding party follows them along the trail of fairy lights, lotus blossoms and silver glitter.

The elephant kneels; Violet and Thea descend. They say their vows, so low-key that there are mutters of dissent among the gathering. Mathilde is having trouble crying. The feathers on the trannies' tails droop. But as soon as the register is signed, the fireworks begin. The brass band resumes, and the congregation becomes a conga line. Josh is clasping the sequined waist of a particularly fine drag queen, grateful that she doesn't have feathers to set off his hayfever. He feels dizzy. He considers slipping out, cooling his cheek against the white tiles in the bathroom. He grabs Mathilde's cigarette from her mouth.

'But you don't smoke,' she says.

'I do tonight.'

SWEDEN

One of the trannies looks familiar. Beneath the arched eyebrows and the cupid bow lips there is the shadow of a boy Josh remembers. Is it Charlie? Charlie Node, his childhood nemesis, his bully? Josh remembers the pine trees, the sensation of bark scratching his cheek. He remembers the threats: Chinese burns, castration, girls' underwear. They never came to anything, except for faked illnesses on Josh's behalf. How funny to see him here. How strange to find him in drag. Maybe it's not him at all. But he's coming nearer.

'I think I might know your brother,' says possibly-Charlie Node.

'No, mate, I . . . ' Now what precisely should he be calling Charlie? Ma'am? 'It's Josh, from school, remember?'

Charlie doesn't seem to remember. 'What was his name?'

'I don't have a brother. We were in the same class together. You and me. When we were about eight.'

'Oh. Right.' Charlie is distracted by a famous person who has arrived fashionably late.

What was that about? What is the point of anything? Josh thinks about how he tries so hard at work, proving himself to all those absent bullies and pricks who ground him down. As if it were some kind of revenge. And they don't even recognise him. Why did Charlie pick on him? Was it just the usual reasons — fucked-up family life, alcoholic father? Or did Charlie sense the malleability in Josh? He doesn't want to think about this; he has recast his thin ply as elegant bentwood furniture. He summons Sweden, scoping for vodka, preferably Absolut.

'Josh, chéri, there you are.'

'Yes,' says Josh, smiling his client presentation smile.

'Meet Chantelle. I was telling Chantelle that her name isn't really French, but she is quite pleased that it is as fake as she.'

Chantelle, or Charlie Node, peals with laughter and flutters her considerable eyelashes.

'Chantelle, meet my boyfriend Josh.'

'Oh, Josh and I have already met. I knew his brother.'

'I don't have a brother.'

'Well, it wasn't you, because his brother was a fag for sure. I can spot them a mile off.'

'Fuck off! I don't have a brother! And he wouldn't be gay if I did!' says Josh.

'Josh! You are such an arsehole! I can't believe I brought you along!' says Mathilde. 'Alors, let's go dance,' she says to Chantelle.

'D'accord, chéri,' says Chantelle.

Josh is alone again. He turns to a woman who is seated beside the lotus pond. She too is dressed in black, an ellipse excised from the back of her gown.

She smiles at Josh. 'Don't tell me, you're an architect, right?'

'Close,' says Josh. 'I'm an industrial designer.'

'It's that turtleneck. And your wire-framed glasses. You all look the same.'

'We do? And what does that make you?' He reaches past her to grab two champagne flutes. He is disturbed to see some of the goldfish floating belly up. He vaguely thinks he should do something. He hands a glass to her.

'Me? I'm an accountant. But don't tell anyone.'

Josh isn't sure how he got home. He hopes Mathilde

didn't drive them. She spent a few years in Paris, and now Josh prays each time she takes a corner.

He hears a clatter of coins. That's right. They came in a taxi. And the taxi wouldn't take a credit card. Or was it that they couldn't find theirs? Had he left his wallet at the wedding? Mathilde is counting in French. 'Soixante-dix-sept, soixante-dix-huit,' she is saying. It is a good thing that he empties his pockets at the door each evening. The man in the polyester shirt and name badge must be the taxi driver.

The coins are transferred, the door is shut. Mathilde walks towards him. 'So who was that woman, cheri? The one with the boring dress?'

'What woman?' He can't remember a woman. Or can he? He sees a lotus blossom, clasped between two white breasts. Mathilde doesn't have a cleavage. 'Oh,' he says.

'Oh? Oh what?'

'An accountant. Un-deux-trois-quatre —' Josh explodes into giggles.

'Merde, an accountant! And the fish, what were you doing with the fish?'

'We were . . . ' Now what was he doing? That's right, he was rescuing them. He was bringing her glasses of mineral water, and she was plopping a fish in each glass. Chantelle/Charlie drank a glass. And didn't he do the Heimlich manoeuvre? His forearms ache; it must be true.

'I saved him. I saved Charlie Node,' Josh says. He feels inordinately pleased with himself, a smile skidding across his face.

'You may have saved Charlie Node, but you broke Chantelle's rib, you salaud.' She kicks his wall. *Pop-crunch!*

'Mathilde, no!' he screams. He grabs her arm but she twists away, kicking along a line of tiles. 'Stupid fucking wall. I hate you, I hate you! Always scratching and bruising me. So white and so boring.'

Josh is brimming with anger, it's erupting: there will be none left over for his prototypes. 'How could you, you bitch? Is this what you think of me?'

She shrugs. '*Bof.*' She punches the tiles at waist level. *Pop-crunch! Pop-crunch!*

The wall is ruined. It taunts him; it reminds him he is on the downward slide. He realises he hates it, like he hates so many things he makes. *Pop-crunch! Pop-crunch!* It's so satisfying, like bursting bubble-wrap.

He and Mathilde lie on the floor, spent. 'Really, it looks much better this way,' she says.

'You think? Hmm, maybe. Like snow-covered volcanos. Like glaciers.'

Josh reaches over to pick up a lily that has hit the ground, and feeds the stem down the front of her dress.

BOOM
the thief
walks away
with the
cash

Double BARREL

1. I'm just going for my fourth plastic cup of fluoro punch when Sol asks me whether I've heard from Thomas.

No, I say. Not for a year at least.

People are always asking me about Thomas. Just because his eyes are set in my son's head they think we have a hold over him. But he doesn't even know.

Last phone call I got he was in Rio de Janeiro, says Sol. Learning about samba.

That makes sense. I remember those sticky nights, sheets peeled back, traffic noises driving through the open window, and Thomas softly beating his fingertips against my ribs, my stomach. Feel this, he'd say. That's salsa, Puerto Rican style. And that — he'd tap my hipbone 1 and 2 and 3 and 1 — that is cumbia.

Says he could do with a gun, says Sol. Says there've been a few dodgy situations.

Oh my god, he's fucking mental, I say. He thought

he needed one here.

Have you met his dad? Says Sol. He's way worse than Thomas. I went out to the farm once with Thomas — just to chill, you know, just to detox a bit — and there he was, trying to fell a pine tree with this mother of a gun called the Avenger. He was going to me, now it's your turn, mate, and I was like, no way man, I've got the shakes as it is, don't want to tear my arm out of its socket.

Sol's wrong. Thomas is worse. The night when Thomas stuck the Smith and Wesson Model 19 revolver in my mouth and whispered its specs — its double-action revolver with swing-out cylinder, its .357 Magnum six-round cylinder with six inch barrel and adjustable notch rear, fixed ramp or partridge front — that was the night that I left. I yanked on my clothes, one sock gone, my underpants lost in the bed tangle, my T-shirt inside out, and ran out, stopping only at the 24-hour service station to buy some Fanta, some gum, anything to get that metal taste out of my mouth.

Thomas thinks Rio's good for the chicks, says Sol. The girls get implants in their butts if they're not big enough. Tall and tan and young and lovely, the girl from Ipanema goes walking — aw, Rosie. I didn't mean anything by that.

Don't apologise, I say, straightening up my five foot five frame, smoothing my skirt with my pale, freckled hand. We're history. I hand Sol my plastic cup, turn and walk out the door. My tits are aching anyway.

2. Here is a farm. A sprawl of grass punctuated by cowpats, threaded with barbed wire, occasioned by cabbage trees. Here is a house, neat and square, white

as a milk tooth, with a long gravel drive that a boy with calloused feet can run down. Here is a clutch of cattle beast, their nose-breath smoking in the cold air, their eyes flashing like they might be bulls in disguise, like they might charge a small boy and gore him, a cheerio on a toothpick, arms and legs flailing as he is paraded on their horns for the day.

Thomas knows that if he had a gun, this could not happen.

He sits in his room at dusk, listening to the ratter-tatter-ratter-tatter of his dad's colt AR-15 and tries to play his Casiotone in time, tries to keep up. Youare-mysunshine, myonlysunshine, youmakemehappy, whenskies are. The gun is too fast. If only he had a snare drum, like the marching band in the Christmas parade. He's heard those drumrolls. They're faster than rain on a tin roof, they're a sea of clapping hands, they're an army of advancing German soldiers in World War II — ratter-tatter-ratter-tatter-ratter — 'Thomas, wash your hands now, dear. It's tea time!'

Thomas lines up eight peas on his plate to make an octave. He inserts five more for the semitones. He plays along to 'Copacabana' on the radio.

'Dad, Thomas is playing with his food,' Raewyn tattle-tales across the table. Such a *good* girl, always helping Mum ice the biscuits and collecting the eggs. Making him look bad. She'll get it.

'Watch it, son. If you're going to treat your mother with such disrespect, there'll be no gun privileges for a week,'

Thomas eats his keyboard. He taps his foot instead. The rhythm is difficult, but by adding his knife he thinks he's nailed it.

'Thomas!'

Thomas stops.

3. Mum's sitting in the living room when I get home, a swaddling of milk stains and baby cries in her arms. You're late, she says. Your son wants a feed.

I left you a bottle, Mum. Couldn't you have given him that?

He won't take the bottle.

Shit. Well, hold on, I'll just get myself ready for bed.

I pull off my tight sparkly top, my frayed jeans, my earrings, my bracelets that would cut into Ziggy's skin. I leave them in the corner of my room, a heap of cigarette and marijuana smells, a trapdoor into my old life. I put on my pyjamas, unbutton them to expose my chewed nipples. I gather Ziggy up, snuggle him close to me, his head resting on my upper arm. For now it feels good; only later will I find that my arm has gone to sleep, tingling and semi-detached. Ziggy suckers himself onto me and I grimace with pain, but it softens. He makes snuffling noises, gulping and dribbling the milk. His fingers and toes press into my not-yet-firm body and I try to justify the vodka, the Drambuie, the whatever else they sloshed into that glass bowl. Ziggy stops sucking and starts crying, and I hate him for not falling asleep. I sit him up and rub his back, massaging out the bubbles of air that cramp his belly. I pull him out of bed to change his nappy and he screams as I wipe off the pumpkin soup poo, as I cream the cracks and origami-wrap his bottom with a triangle of cotton. I lie him on the bed and go to wash my hands. My mother peeks through her yellow door sliver and asks if everything is okay, do I need her to jiggle him because he's making an awful racket.

No, Mum, I say through gritted teeth, because sometimes when I am holding him and he is crying, she will take him from me and he will be quiet. He prefers her to me; he knows I think he's an imposition.

I dry my hands on the damp, threadbare handtowel and go back to my bedroom. I pick up the squalling boy and lie him beside me again. I expose my other breast, which doesn't hurt nearly as much as the first, and he tugs the milk out of me, a magician's scarf that keeps unfurling.

4. Thomas is thinking about Rio de Janeiro. Despite everything, he wishes he was there. It's cold in the New York City subway, and no matter how fast he beats on his assortment of upturned plastic buckets he cannot quicken his blood. Sometimes an audience gathers around him, tapping their feet, tossing their shrapnel into his fedora, but he knows how meaningless this is, because he sees the same copper pennies scattered all over the footpath. When he first arrived he would gather them all up, thinking each one was a piece of luck. But then the coffee and donut cart guy told him not to collect the tails-up pennies or his good luck would run out. Now the streets have frozen over, and his fingers are clumsy in their gloves, and besides, all the heads are gone.

The Q train pulls in and the doors open to a puff of heat. People ignore Thomas's latticework of rhythms, kicking his buckets in their rush to get up the steps.

'Hey, watch it!' he yells, but he doesn't have his father's command.

He doesn't know how much longer he can take this. He says hi to the people he shares the stage with but he thinks they have an underworld quality about them. There's the emaciated old man with long white hair who plays the electric organ for a troupe of invisible dancing monkeys. And there's the woman in a blue suit who holds her *Watchtower* magazines with mute appeal, each heralding another tragedy. Aids deaths, child slave labour, demonic possession, nuclear war. The Quechua Indians play their pan-pipes and charangos out of tune. Were they even musicians in their home town? They funnel sorrow through their instruments. At least their ponchos keep them warm.

And what do people make of Thomas? A talented musician doing whatever it takes to be discovered by one of those execs who work in the neighbourhood? Or just another deluded no-hoper, a junkie who can't keep a day job?

'Hey, man, time's up.' Someone claps him on the shoulder. 'My turn now.' Thomas scans the tall black man for gun-shaped mounds. He can't see any.

'Uh, okay, just let me pack up.' He's surprised he's managed to play here for as long as he has; these public thoroughfares have property laws all of their own. He grabs his fedora and stacks his plastic buckets, watching as the man pulls two bongos out of his zip bag. Thomas shivers. The man settles himself on his own upturned bucket. He rubs and blows on his hands, then coaxes out a salsa rhythm. Thomas sits down on the bench, organising his coins by kind.

'Watcha doin', hangin' about? I ain't goin' nowhere.'

'I'm just listening. You're good.'

'Uh huh.'

'Are you Puerto Rican?' He's getting better at guessing people's origins.

'My mom is.' He closes his eyes, bites his lip, sinks beneath the beats, filling the concrete tunnel with more rhythm than one person can make. It's like he's slapping the ceilings, the trains, the stairs, the rails with his hands. Even the rats pause to listen. 'And my girl is,' he says as he reins it in. 'That makes my son three-quarters Puerto Rican.' The rhythm shifts a little, and Thomas can hear 'Oye como va'. He resists the urge to sing. 'You got kids?'

'Ah, no?' says Thomas.

'You don't sound so sure about that.'

'Well, there was this girl I knew before I left. A mate says she's got a baby now. The timing's right. But she could have been whoring around.'

'In God we trust. You can count on rhythm as well. But bitches? You never know. I'd kill the mothafucka who touched my girl.' He quickens his hands, pulling the song out from under Thomas's feet. '"Tall and tan and young" — you wanna kid?'

'Only if it's mine.'

'Then it's yours. Ciao.' He closes his eyes. Dismissed.

Thomas tallies the stack of coins. There's about three dollars. He's going to have trouble covering his rent. And what can three dollars buy? A congealed piece of pizza, a bagel that's long since lost its charm? He considers scouring the rubbish bins; they throw away so much good food here. But he's not that far gone yet.

5. Sol is sitting on his marbled black vinyl bar stool in Drum King. He's tapping away at the glass counter with a blue biro to Rosie's riff, which plays in his head. He wonders whether she's picked up the guitar since Ziggy was born. Probably not: she's back at her mum's and her mum likes Glen Campbell.

There goes Rosie now. Funny that, right after he was thinking about her. She's like royalty — the music precedes her. She's pushing her pram past the mosaic-tiled wall on her way to the fruit shop, or maybe The Warehouse. Why hasn't she stopped in to say hi?

'Rosie! Rosie!' he yells, and his voice causes the cymbals to shimmer. She doesn't hear.

Sol runs outside. 'Hey, Rosie!' She stops and turns, shielding her eyes from the sun.

'Oh, hi, Sol,' she calls. He flicks over the *Back in five minutes* sign, pulls the shop door shut behind him and crosses the road to talk to her.

She looks different with the baby. Somehow softer and paler. She's wearing a baggy jersey and jeans, not the usual figure-hugging numbers she wears to parties and gigs. Her freckles float on her luminescent skin, and her eyelashes are glass noodles without mascara. The effect isn't off-putting, though.

The baby is asleep underneath a black sun visor, and when Sol goes to lift the corner to take a peek, Rosie tells him off. 'Let him sleep. He was awake for five hours, and he was beside himself.'

'Sorry,' says Sol. And he is. Sorry that this is Thomas's son, and that Thomas is too up his arse to register the fact. Thomas is his mate, but really. How could he let Rosie go? And how could such a fuckup manage to get his shit together, get out of this hell-hole suburban drum shop, find himself in New York City?

'Did someone just go into your shop?' Rosie asks.

Damn. He forgot to snib the lock. 'Hey, nice seeing you again, Rosie. You should stop by for a jam sometime. Bring the baby.'

She nods and waves as he runs over the road, tries to open the door. It's locked. There *is* someone inside, walking towards the counter. Sol rummages in his pockets for the keys, wedged underneath his wallet. He unlocks the door but by this time the bastard's in the till.

Sol digs into his other pocket, looking for his cellphone. 'Get out of my store,' he hears his voice squeak. 'I'm calling the cops.' The cellphone isn't there. It's on the counter next to the thief. Sol looks at it, and the thief follows his eyes and snickers, all the time stuffing the cash into his pockets. Sol has just sold a drum kit for $1200, and the buyer, gang-patched and tattooed, paid in cash. He was going to take it to the bank, but that was before Rosie walked by.

Sol looks around for a weapon. The crappy marked-down Japanese snare drum — that'll do. He grabs it, lifts it over his head.

But the thief has found Thomas's gun. Sol's been looking after it. It was in the back of the till, underneath all the cheques and the Visa slips. He points it at Sol, bites his bottom lip.

'Don't bother, it's not loaded,' says Sol.

The thief clicks back the safety catch with an incredulous look, spins the .357 Magnum six-round cylinder and pulls the trigger. Sol drops the snare drum in front of him and, as the bullet bursts through the membrane, he observes that the sound quality isn't nearly as tinny as he remembered, and perhaps he should have picked up the table instead. The bullet lodges in his stomach with a quiet thuck. As Sol plops down on the drum stool, his foot hits the bass pedal. *Boom*. The thief walks away with the cash. Sol slides to the floor.

6. This is what Thomas dreams. He's in the carnival, a bongo hanging around his neck. He is naked, his flesh painted blue like an Indian deity. Only when he tries to rub some of the blue away he realises that he has been tattooed. He is playing a samba beat but his fingers have become putty. Every time they slap the drum they stretch and fall off. And then they are around him. Like they were that day, their eyebrows arched halfway up their foreheads, their false eyelashes tarantula legs. Their muscular exfoliated thighs bursting out of their fishnets, their naked butts morphing from soft to hard with each platform-heeled step. Their fingernails are in Thomas's flesh; they have pierced his drum.

You think you got rhythm? You silly boy! You cannot play, you cannot play one little bit. And then they've pulled him out of the parade, into that room, with its naked lightbulb and fresh-fruit calendar, with its stained carpet. They tape his genitals up into his groin, they platinum wig his head. But there is no money or passport to steal from his naked body. Instead there is a giant American hole punch, with three holes rather than two.

But I am not American! Thomas cries, like he did that day. I am not American! They slide his body in between the metal, then they all sit on the lever, their bums flattening. Bang. Three holes. Like his sister. They shift him. Bang. Another three holes. Nine, twelve, fifteen. And then he is standing there, watching the rest of the carnival go by, listening to 'Copacabana' piping through his perforated body.

7. I hear the gunshot as I pick up a mango with a *Product of Brazil* sticker. When I open my eyes to all those people's faces peering down at me it is still in my hand, its juice is dribbling down my wrist. I sit up, look around. My heart almost stops again. Where's my baby? I ask. Where's Ziggy?

My daughter, she have him, says the older Cambodian woman who runs this shop. And there she is, outside, rocking the pushchair. I rush over to comfort Ziggy, to gather him up in my arms, but he is still sleeping. What happened? I ask the daughter.

The drum shop man, he shot, she says, pointing over the road. And there is an ambulance, and medics, with someone — is it Sol? — strapped to the stretcher. I leave Ziggy with the daughter and run across the road. I push my way through the gaggle.

Sol? I say.

Excuse me, miss, are you next of kin?

They check his pulse, they put on an oxygen mask, they heave him into the open doors of the ambulance. And then I am shoved into the crowd by the police, who are readjusting their barrier tape. I am nobody: just another rubber-necker. I cross the road to reclaim Ziggy and it's not until I have pushed him home that I realise that all I have from the fruit shop is a stolen mango.

8. All through the next day Thomas can't shake that dream. He keeps glancing down, surprised when he can't see the sifting crowd through the holes in his abdomen. The funny thing is, the mugging wasn't a big deal. Their gun didn't scare him; he'd already seen the worst happen. Sure, it was a pain in the arse trying to get a new passport, but he had photocopies and extra cash in the hotel room, and the consulate wasn't hard to find. It hurt like hell getting the tape off, but afterwards the pain was exhilarating, a hit of speed. The bitter aftertaste is what they said about his drumming. *You branco, the rhythm, it come from your head. How can you play when you don't feel? Are you a man? Where are your balls?*

Today he has his audition. He saw an ad in the *Village Voice*, decided to follow it up — who knows, maybe get a regular gig indoors, with a semi-regular paycheck. But how can he convince anyone with those voices ricocheting around his head?

If he had had a gun, that would shut them up. He longs for one like a junkie. He'd like to feel its shaft slipping along his inner thigh, stiffening him slightly as he walks down the street.

But he's trying to give all that up. Why did his mum keep the guns when his dad went to prison? It's her fault what he did to Rosie. Rosie, Rosie, the only girl he ever really connected with. But he ruined all that, didn't he? Doesn't matter if she's had his child, if the rumours are true. Would she want a potential serial-killer as the father of her child?

He's got to submerge himself in music. That's been his life's defence. That's how he's faced his dad's absence, his mum's muteness, his sister's empty room after she was mistaken for a wild pig in the bush. He used to practise his drums in there. He'd make her dusty dolls dance on their shelves. Until his mum would yank him out and shut the door. He thought that room would make a great studio but, like the guns, she couldn't let it go.

9. I've been sitting here for an hour, singing to Ziggy so that he doesn't cry, but also singing to Sol. I'm giving his mum a break; the poor woman looks like she hasn't slept in days. Sol looks different: all pale and covered in wires. He's had a blood transfusion and I wonder whether he's different now, with someone else's cells coursing through his body. Will his rhythm change? Will he now like fried chicken instead of pinto beans? Ziggy starts to kvetch; I start another. 'Her name was Lola, she was a show girl . . . ' but it's quite the wrong song and I stop.

10. Thomas can't tell whether the person who answers the door is a man or a woman. The stature suggests a man, and when he shakes the outstretched hand his suspicions are confirmed. But she introduces herself as Melissa. Come on through, she says. Would you like a drink? Coffee? Soda? Oh, and I've also got a pitcher of sangría, even though winter's hardly the time for it. But it's so warm in this apartment, who's to say what season it is?

She sashays into the living room, which is also the bedroom and the kitchen. It is a large space and the light that floods through the windows reminds him of movies he has seen.

Yeah, a sangría would be nice, Thomas says. Anything

to loosen this anxiety.

So, tell me about yourself, Melissa calls from the kitchen alcove. You have a cute accent.

Oh, thanks. Thomas finds this observation strange; he was taught to believe that it was nasal and lazy. I'm from New Zealand. I've been here for a few months now. Before that I was in Brazil. Learning about samba.

Oh, samba, how wonderful. Did you have a teacher there?

No, not really. I just hung out a lot, went to some bars, took part in the carnival. It was pretty wild. Kinda dangerous as well. I got mugged by some tra — Thomas looks at Melissa and stops. Some guys. So I thought I should try somewhere new, but maybe I left too soon.

What, you don't like it here in the greatest city on earth?

I didn't say that.

I hear you, sugar. New York is a very unforgiving city. You shoulda seen me when I first arrived. All big feet and hairy wrist bones, wearing this terrible nylon wig and a stained pink suit I had stolen from my ex-wife. Luckily this old queen gave me a place in her finishing school, taught me about silicon makeup and electrolysis, what it takes to be a lady.

Your ex-wife?

Oh, I was real young; I thought I could change who I was. Clueless, huh? But I got a daughter now — that I don't regret. You want to see a photo?

Sure.

Melissa pulls out a picture of a girl, maybe eleven or twelve. She's all dark hair and big eyes, revealing her braces to the camera. Thomas shudders: there's something about his sister in the photo. And he thought he had stopped seeing her everywhere.

She's pretty, he says.

So, do you want to hear what I do? Melissa asks. She doesn't wait for an answer but she starts to sing. Her voice is hoarse and sweet, with diva swoops into falsetto. She sounds like something in between Nina Simone and Lou Reed. But it's more than the sound that causes ice to skate down Thomas's spine, that cocks the hair follicles on his scalp. She's scooping the song out of a bowl of pain, unhooking it from a thorn bush, and it's not just hers, it's his mother's lost voice; it's Thomas's too.

When she's done, Thomas just sits there.

You're crying — oh, sweetheart, I just love it when I make that happen.

I'm — (not crying), he was going to say. But instead he accepts the handkerchief, which is edged with forget-me-nots and has the initial R. embroidered on it. Rosie. And Raewyn, his sister's name. A coincidence, he knows, but enough of one that he completely loses it, loses himself.

He never cries — this is not him with trails of snot, this is not Thomas who was beside his dad on the day, mud smeared on his face, not crying, even after it happened. This is not Thomas who has a six foot four transvestite's arm around his shoulder saying There, there, it's all right, let it all out, sugar, I'm flattered, honestly.

When he has all dried up and laughed at a few more stories about Melissa's first days in New York City, she asks him if he would like to play for her.

Okay, he says. He looks at his hands; they don't seem

to be shaking. He unzips his bongos, the ones he bought in Brazil, and wedges them between his knees. He thinks of a song, Rosie's song, and he starts layering the beats up over it until it is transformed, it is a carnival in itself. And as he drums, his fingers falling faster than rain on a tin roof, he sees his sister's smocked dresses puff up with dancing ghosts, he hears the wind-chime tinkling like there's a tornado in her room. He plays the way he can only play when he is entirely alone.

And then it's over. He looks at Melissa, who is appraising him — not crying like he did, but still, something has shifted.

I think you'll do just fine, she says. You free next Tuesday?

11. It is heavy under water, knotted in seaweed. Sol tries to unclasp the clamshells, unravel the octopus legs, but they hold him tight. Through the aquamarine undulations he can hear a familiar song. He strains to make out the tune, but it is fading: the sound of his heartbeat is drowning it out.

12. Thomas walks home, beside himself with excitement. The door has opened; the dresses and dolls can dance out of his sister's bedroom. Before, he was playing stolen riffs from favourite records. Now, he can interpret the miasma inside his head.

He thinks about taking the train — it is still too cold, too grey out here. But his blood is thrumming and glowing enough to keep him warm, and besides, he has so much energy to burn he would go crazy having to sit still for ten minutes.

He is making good progress; already he has passed Canal Street, just a few more blocks south and east. Melissa said she had a gig booked in the East Village, and it would pay: Thomas would be able to make his rent this month. Though why he should have to shell out so much to sleep on some mate's brother's infested futon is beyond him. The landlord doesn't heat the place properly, and the stove doesn't work. He passes a man sitting in a pee-soaked box; he reminds himself that he is lucky. Lucky, lucky, lucky, after all this freakin' time. He wants to talk to someone, but who? He doesn't know anyone here yet, unless you count the coffee and donut cart man, or the Puerto Rican in the subway.

He passes a phone box. He could call someone. Not his mum and dad — they'd give him shit for not calling sooner. He'd like to call Rosie; he wants to ask if it's true. But she'd probably hang up on him. Maybe Sol. Sol would be happy for him — he shares the music passion. He hopes Sol can join him here one day, when Thomas is a celebrated percussionist, written up in all the magazines. He'll have a Soho apartment with a light-flooded music studio, a guest suite. Sol can stay as long as he likes. They'll drink a beer and share takeout from Thomas's favourite Vietnamese, and Sol will be amazed at how chilled Thomas is, how untwitchy, how totally bullet-detoxed. Thomas will give Sol some phone numbers to call, and Sol will get a gig within days. He'll hug Thomas, tell him he's the best friend a bloke could have, not a fuckup after all. And then Sol will call Rosie, tell her how changed Thomas is, and she will decide to visit with her little boy. Thomas will shout them the airfare; he'll paint a room blue.

Thomas opens his wallet to extract his telephone numbers. He pulls out his phone card and punches in the endless stream of numbers to connect to New Zealand for a cut-rate call. He stomps the pavement; he can't feel his toes. Melissa smiles inside him: everything's gonna be all right, sugar. Don't you worry a bit.

The phone starts to ring.

Hello?

The accent sounds exaggerated, so out of context. Hey, says Thomas, is Sol there?

Oh, haven't you heard? says the girl, maybe Sol's sister. He's in hospital. Still unconscious.

What happened? says Thomas, his heart racing.

Some guy busted into the shop and shot him with this gun he found in the till.

What kind of gun?

I dunno — how do you expect me to know that? Look, do you want me to take a message or what? We're reading them out to Sol anyway; the doctor thinks that he might be able to hear stuff.

Uh, no, don't worry about it.

Who are you anyway? If you're the arsehole who did it, if this is some sick way of seeing the damage you've done, you've got something coming to you, mate.

No! No, no. I'm just an old friend. Thomas, all right? Tell Sol Thomas called.

Thomas, says the girl, like a penny's dropping, and it's not going to land heads up. Did you —

Thomas hangs up the phone quickly; he cannot bear to hear the accusation. It might have been his gun. But Sol wouldn't have taken it to work, would he? Sol would have put it in a safe deposit box; he's got a good head on his shoulders.

He knows things like that happen all the time in the States, but in New Zealand?

Oh god, oh no, he can feel it happening: the lead, it's entering his bloodstream, his stomach is an empty six-round cylinder. He-needs-a-gun, he-needs-a-gun, there-is-a-gun-shop-two-blocks-away, he could go west, not east, there is a pawnshop four blocks south, it would be so easy, then he could shoot something, anything, those damn rats, that damn futon, his foot, he fuckin' hates himself, if only he could tear himself apart, how could he, how could he, how could he let all of this happen?

13. Sol opened his eyes earlier today. I wasn't there; I was at the park with Ziggy. Ziggy likes the swings, I push him back and forth and he giggles and we look like we're out of a nappy advertisement. When we get to the hospital his mother tells me the news — the doctor says it will happen again and maybe next time he'll wake for ten minutes. Sol's mother hugs me. She's got the wrong idea: she thinks I'm his girlfriend. She's hoping she's Ziggy's grandmother. She doesn't know it was all my fault. If I had not stopped to talk, if I had not pointed out the man in his shop, if I had not run from Thomas, then would things have turned out differently? Maybe.

I sit and I watch Sol's eyelashes. They tremor slightly: his eyes are moving, they surface like fish. He's dreaming. His brain is alive. I pick a few grapes from the bowl, delivered by the fruit shop even though he is not conscious to enjoy them. The skins are tough; they have thickened in their journey across the Pacific. The juice splurts out and slaps Sol on the cheek. He stirs.

Ziggy has fallen asleep on my chest, and I am dozing too. But then:

Rosie?

I grunt, I start.

Rosie, I hear again. The waters have broken. Sol is coming.

Sol, I say. I reach out my finger and place it on his lips.

She was wearing
1960s diamanté-
studded glasses

AUTO IMMUNE

'Voglie comprare un cocodrillo?' I asked Camilla. She had declared herself Italian and didn't want us to take her elegant black coat. She wrapped it around her Picasso angles. Her nose was particularly cubist, in opposition to her jutting chin. Her teeth jostled one another. But none of those things made her ugly.

'You speak Italian?'

'Un pocissimo,' I said. 'I studied it in my first year of university.' My tongue wouldn't trill or sigh, and I could never remember which consonant was hard or soft, so I swapped to film studies, and fooled myself that I understood *La Dolce Vita* without the subtitles.

'And what about you? What do you study?' she asked Daniel, who was perched on the roll-armed chair that bloomed frayed roses. It came from his mother's house, a facsimile of an English country manor.

'Art history,' he said. 'Botticelli, Titian, Raphael,

Michelangelo, Caravaggio. I think I might do my honours in the Italian Renaissance.'

Camilla ran her eyes along the leg of Daniel's black trousers and up his turtleneck, taking in his square-framed glasses, his tightly curled hair. 'But you dress like an Italian. That is unusual among New Zealand men.'

Daniel blushed and I felt proud. I had discovered him in the back of my Art History 101 tutorial. His limbs were still a drawer of mismatched cutlery, his glasses unfashionably large. I had helped him pick out new ones. I had found his jacket in an op-shop, and he had had it dry-cleaned, replaced its torn lining with aubergine satin.

We both loved garage sales. Every Saturday morning we met at our local café and put rings around classified advertisements. I navigated as Daniel drove his baby blue Mini, always parked on hills to help it start. We complemented each other: he reached for the antiques and I for the kitsch. We decided to get a flat together.

'Uh, thanks,' Daniel said, smiling at Camilla. 'And why are you here in New Zealand?'

'I am studying the Italian fishing community in Island Bay. Maybe for my Masters, maybe for my PhD. I'll see how it goes.'

Daniel gave me the look he reserved for under-priced Royal Doulton sugar bowls. I nodded in assent. The other candidates seemed potato-ish in comparison. Why ask whether she cooked and cleaned, why ask what kind of appliances she could contribute? Why scan her taste in music or books? Daniel cleared his throat.

'Would you like to move in? The room is free now; you can come anytime.'

Camilla walked to the fireplace in her impossibly

narrow boots. She scrutinised the arrow-pierced Saint Sebastian, his blood thick globs of oil paint, his neck tense in ecstatic agony. The legs were too thick, the toga did not ripple like the original, but it was a convincing copy.

'You paint this?' She looked at me, then at Daniel.

'Yes,' Daniel said. 'I'm not very good.'

'But you are!' She stretched out her finger to feel the blood. 'Okay,' she said. 'I move in.'

We shook hands and then she kissed us on the cheek. 'Relax, I am not going to bite you. We live together now, why be so reserved?'

We watched from the step as she opened the passenger door of a car. I thought I glimpsed a balding head with a ponytail. The car definitely had a spoiler.

We didn't know the house was damp when we found it in summer. The walls were not yet slicked with condensation; our clothes hadn't grown mildew. We were charmed by the glorious views, all the inlets and seas, the upward arrows of villa roofs set into the green hills. We loved the chunkiness of the 1920s architecture, its unchanged kitchen with the heavy cupboards and drawers, its portico into the dining room through which you could pass gravy-boats and tureens. The bathroom had mosaic black and white tiles on the floor, octagons set together in chiaroscuro blooms. The living room had a bay window and an alcove into which Daniel slid his piano. He propped Gilbert and Sullivan on the music stand but he kept the lid shut as the trip up the path had knocked it out of tune.

On sunny days he would sit smoking on the stone

steps. He invited me to join him, but I didn't want to take up cigarettes. He was joined by our former flatmate, Jenny, who was happy to blow smoke rings and talk about keg parties. I didn't like the rugby-loving 'Dan' he became with her.

Jenny left, not bothering with two weeks' notice. We put it down to the dishes situation, but Daniel ran into a friend of hers who explained. Jenny had run off with a mortgage broker for whom she worked part time. He was twice her age — he had a daughter just a few years younger than Jenny. Everyone was scandalised, so they eloped to Levin.

Camilla moved in the next weekend. A tall, slack-bellied man in white ankle socks heaved a suitcase up the stairs. He was the owner of the lank ponytail. Camilla bumped up another case, shoes bursting from its zip. She was wearing 1960s diamanté-studded glasses, and the corners of her black bob stabbed the air. The man balanced a futon on his head, shuffling down the hall like a pantomime horse.

I had the room with a view, in exchange for relinquishing communal decorating decisions to Daniel. It was painted the pink of my childhood antibiotics. There were roses on the carpet. I enhanced it with all my pink garage sale finds: my bakelite radio, my pearlescent brush and mirror set, my china swan, the frou-frou chair I had covered with pink fake fur. From the windows you could see the harbour and the South Coast. Daniel and Camilla's rooms faced the bank. I sat at my desk, trying to read my university set texts. I would get distracted by the sun that abandoned us mid-morning to woo

Mt Victoria.

I didn't like the hall. I ran down it when I had to go to the loo in the middle of the night, and it seemed that something hovered in the high ceilings, its claws clicking against the fuse box. The night Daniel told me his séance and dead-headmaster-visitation stories over a bottle of red wine, and then switched off the mains as a prank, I screamed and didn't stop until all the lights were turned on and the gin was pulled out from under Daniel's bed. We didn't have any tonic so we drank it straight.

Daniel suspected that his room was haunted too. He had a dream that might not have been one. A fern was tapping against the window, its coil of new growth like a soft club. He opened his eyes and there, sitting on the end of the bed, were two young girls, dressed in lace-edged white linen. They were pale, their hair rag-ringleted, drawn from their faces by black velvet ribbons. He pulled his Liberty print duvet over his head and when he next woke they were gone.

We hadn't told Camilla about the ghosts at the interview; in fact, we hadn't discussed much at all. We found her on the sofa in the living room, her legs thrown over the ponytailed man. It seemed all wrong: she ought to be with someone dark and angular, wearing a sharp suit.

'Hi, I'm Hugh,' he said, stretching out his hand.

'Hi. Naomi,' I replied.

''Ugo is my friend from Italy,' Camilla said.

'Really?' He didn't seem Italian.

'We met last year when I was over teaching English,' explained Hugh.

'You think that a man lives in Italy, he learn some style. But no, 'Ugo is *soooo* unfashionable. It is because he is cheap.'

'Oh,' I said, giggling apologetically at the truth.

'In Italy, you can buy the olive oil. The first pressing is best. Then there is the second pressing, the third pressing. After all the oil is gone, they press the stones. That is the worst. That is what 'Ugo buy.' She poked him in the ribs. Hugh smiled at her indulgently.

'So do you have olive oil?' Camilla asked me.

'I don't think so. We have sunflower oil.'

'We have to go shopping then. What meat shall we have tonight?'

'None, this is a vegetarian flat.'

'Vegetarian? But why?' Camilla looked confused.

'We just are.' I ate fish, but I had given up red meat along with Italian classes. The thought of blood soaking the breadboard made me squeamish.

'You did not tell me that before I move in. But you need some meat, Naomi. You look so pale.'

I smiled. 'Great.' I liked being pale. I had a pink Chinese parasol for summer, and sometimes I even wore gloves.

I feared shopping trips. The last time Daniel and I went, his nails had left a row of crescent moons in my wrist over a loaf of bread. I had wanted toast slice; he thought that sandwich was more economical. He thought I ate too much bread and turned the heater on too often. His domestic austerity offset his extravagance when it came to antiques and cigarettes. He ate mince pies and burgers downtown, glad that the flat kitty wasn't to be frittered on meat.

But it was different with Camilla. 'We buy anchovies, yes? And we must buy the Italian pasta. Oh, and parmesan. No, not in that tube. What is that, dry skin? And Nutella, yes.'

'Nutella?' said Daniel. The hazelnut spread didn't seem Italian enough for him to allow.

'No, Nut-elllllllll-la. It is a double l. You must emphasise it. Like Cam-illllll-la.'

'Right.' We had been mispronouncing her name. The jar went into the trolley.

'I cook for you tonight,' she promised, adding broccoli and some garlic bulbs, perusing the next aisle for a bottle of extra virgin olive oil.

'$12 for this?' said Daniel. He stared wistfully at the budget vegetable oil, two litres for only $3.

'Aah, you are like 'Ugo.'

Daniel grimaced and adjusted the line of his trousers.

Camilla had brought a giant pot like the one my mother boiled her pickle jars in. She filled it up with water. When it boiled, she poured a steady stream of salt into the bubbles. I watched, eager to learn her ways.

'Are you sure you should put so much salt in?' I asked.

'Yes, of course, because the water must move fast so the pasta does not stick.'

She broke off a floret of broccoli, separated it into slivers, and peeled a clove of garlic. She didn't cut it up. She removed two anchovies from the tin and swooshed the bottom of the frying pan with olive oil. When the pasta went into the pot, she sautéed her pinch of ingredients. Then she drained the pasta and tossed it all together, serving it up on four plates.

We sat in front of the television with our dinner on our laps. Hugh sat in Daniel's mother's chair, snorting at the sitcom. Daniel frowned, and pulled out his piano stool. We looked down at the pasta. There wasn't any sauce on it. I had got one little piece of broccoli and I couldn't see any anchovy. Daniel had got the clove of garlic and was prodding it. The pasta was chewy, almost uncooked. Daniel and I had previously discussed how you tell when pasta was ready. Daniel said that if you threw it at the wall, it should stick. But what would he know? We both had been raised on meat and potatoes. This was what al dente really meant. I bit down on my disappointment.

'So what do you think of New Zealand food?' I asked.

Camilla rolled her eyes. 'Your lasagne, it is terrible. It is pasta pie! And I went to a friend's place, he made me pizza with spaghetti and pineapple on it. It was disgusting! But your wine, is not so bad.' She poured herself another glass, topping up ours too. 'But I don't understand, why you eat in front of television? In Italy, meals are important. We sit around a table, we talk about the food, we laugh. Here, you eat, you are quiet. You are sooo cold and wet, like your country. Where is the life?'

Daniel and I looked at each other. 'I didn't grow up eating in front of the television,' I said. 'We sat around the kitchen table until my mum broke it by slamming down the cast-iron frying pan.'

'Okay,' said Camilla, not sure whether this contradicted her theory. 'Your mother, she was angry?'

'By dinnertime, usually. But also Dad wasn't a very good furniture-maker.'

AUTO IMMUNE

'After my father left we ate dinner in front of the news,' said Daniel. I sat forward, eager for Daniel's elusive childhood. 'We had trays with bean-filled cushions under them, so they would stay level. We didn't have a remote, so you couldn't mute it during the ad breaks. But I liked it that way; she couldn't complain to me what a worthless cheat Dad was.'

Camilla looked concerned. 'How Anglo-Saxon you New Zealanders are. Where was the love?'

'My mother loved me,' said Daniel in a small voice.

For once, I didn't dwell on Daniel. I smarted. I wasn't a cold, wet Anglo-Saxon; I was of Irish descent. I hugged my friends hello, I had been to protests, I had smashed my favourite Carltonware plate in fury, I had cried when the heroine died in *La Traviata*. Couldn't she see the fire in my belly?

'It is chilly, I turn on the heater.'

Daniel tensed; he wanted to say something but he didn't. He watched as Camilla switched both bars on, then fetched the fan heater from her bedroom and plugged that in too.

Camilla left with Hugh that night, and Daniel and I whispered, fearing she might catch us talking about her.

'Why is she with that man?' asked Daniel. 'He's a disaster. A banker? How dull. And he's so unattractive — what can she see in him?'

'He's got a car,' I pointed out. 'And he's probably rich.'

'But she's so striking. I'd love to paint her. Maybe in a long black velvet gown, a side profile. Anything to get that nose in. And a glimpse of fang: do you think she'd make a good vampire?'

'No, not tall enough.' Why was Daniel showing such

enthusiasm for her? He should realise where his loyalties lay. She wouldn't have said he dressed like an Italian if it weren't for me. He would still be a geek, relegated to the stinky Dungeons and Dragons club. I was sure we were meant to be together. He had held my hand when we went to see the glowworms at the Botanic Gardens. His lips had grazed my ear as he whispered to me at the opera. It would only have been a matter of turning my face to him. But I had been scared.

'Maybe he was better looking in Italy,' I suggested. 'Maybe he's gone to seed since he came home.'

'Doubt it. But Camilla, she's wonderful,' said Daniel, pouring the remains of Hugh and Camilla's glasses into his own. 'I hope she stays.'

'Yeah, so do I.' She *was* rude, *and* she was exciting. But her tiny feet made mine feel bigger; her black hair made mine seem more beige. I was not exotic. I was not exalted. I was just there.

When I woke the next morning I had red spots all over my body. Was I allergic to anchovies? I tried to get up but I felt dizzy so I lay down again.

I woke later that day. When I looked at my stomach I saw that the spots had grown. They were now poppies, growing in the field of my flesh. I climbed very slowly out of bed.

The hall was a no-man's-land and the bathroom tiles slapped the soles of my feet. I went to wash my face, but when I looked in the mirror I was different. My lips had swollen, my cheeks were round and scarlet where they had previously concaved beneath my cheekbones.

I slumped against the bathroom door. I must have

passed out because I awoke to thumping.

'Naomi? You in there?'

It was Daniel. I winched myself up on the towel rail and turned the handle.

'What the hell has happened to you?' Daniel said.

'I don't know.'

'You should go to the doctor.'

'Yes, but how?' I said. I didn't think I had the energy to walk down the hall.

'I'll drive you.'

'Okay,' I said. I was grateful for the offer, even though I hated him seeing me this way. I pressed my face into the seatbelt as we rolled silently down the hill. Then the engine lurched and the Mini ground its way forward.

'Hmmm,' said the doctor, examining the raised blooms on my torso, which were now the size of bread and butter plates. 'I think this may be a case of erythema multiforme. Auto-immune. Your body is turning on itself. I'll do some blood tests to confirm, but I think this will probably have to be treated with a course of steroids. Do you mind if I invite some of my colleagues in? For a learning experience: we don't normally see this one outside of textbooks.'

I nodded; I didn't think I had a choice.

He opened the door. 'Nurse! Dr Paton! Dr Smythe! Come and have a look at this.'

The doctor's colleagues trickled in.

'How fascinating,' said Dr Smythe.

'Quite spectacular,' said Dr Paton.

'Gosh, it's pretty, isn't it? Are you itchy, dear?' asked the nurse.

'Yes I am.' I was startled by the sympathy.

'You're going to need lots of bed rest,' the doctor concluded after his colleagues had left. 'Tar baths will reduce the irritation. And make sure your room is warm. I know these miserable student flats — rising damp has a lot to answer for.'

I lay in bed. At times I stared down at myself, expecting poppies to burst from my pyjamas, looking for their discarded hairy sacs. Daniel had brought in the heater and turned on a bar, and the condensation slowly evaporated, the walls drying along with my lips.

I slipped in and out of sleeping. I thought I heard the ghost claws scratching at my door. I looked for the girls with ringlets but they did not visit this room. I absorbed Daniel and Camilla's words and smoke that wafted through my window. It seemed that Camilla liked rugby too. I interpreted the silences as kisses, and my poppies burned. Sometimes Daniel would bring me in pieces of toast and weak tea and, as the door opened, the hall would be bright and full of laughter. Camilla came to see me as well; she brought me a bowl of golden garlic soup and then told me she and Daniel were going to a club, and hopefully there would be dancing, because in Italy she liked to dance till dawn. Did I know anyone who sold marijuana? Was there anywhere that played Latin music? Daniel preferred Gregorian; he didn't know.

That night I got up and sat in the empty living room, staring at the points where the arrows entered Saint Sebastian's wounds. My poppies had faded; my skin was like a piece of ageing stained paper. I missed its vividness; I disliked the awareness that my mending body brought.

I stood to go back to my room, but paused at Camilla's door. Her room was austere. Her futon didn't have a base, and her line of shoes was the principal decoration. Clothes spilt out of her suitcase, not yet unpacked. I moved on to Daniel's room. His floor was a tangle of dirty clothes and men's magazines; on his shelves there were cologne bottles, comic books and half-eaten sandwiches. It belied his suaveness, and again I wondered what it was about him that eluded me. I lay down on his bed, pulling his duvet across me. I looked at all the Italian Renaissance martyrs he had painted, bleeding in their garage sale gilt frames. I watched the fern tapping on the window, and climbed its green ladder of fronds to the gauzy moon.

'Naomi. Naomi!' Someone was shaking my shoulder. I opened my eyes. 'What are you doing here?'

'I wanted to see the girls.'

'What girls?'

'The ones with the ringlets and the white dresses.'

'What are you talking about? Go back to bed.'

Daniel led me to my room like a small child, and tucked me in. He bent over to kiss me, and I inclined my lips, but instead he kissed my patchy forehead. He left the room and closed the door.

We went out to a bar to celebrate my return to health. Camilla seemed to know everyone there, even though she had only been in New Zealand for about four months. She kissed their cheeks and flirted. I pointed out that her jeans were unbuttoned, but she shrugged and pushed out her lower lip. She didn't button them up, and I decided it was an Italian fashion. Or maybe she'd put on weight. Daniel chatted to the man pouring the drinks, and I felt annoyed that neither of them was paying attention to me. I was the inspiration for the outing. Then again, they were probably going out anyway.

'Where's Hugh?' I asked when Camilla returned to our table.

'He doesn't like to drink. He has work in the morning; sooo boring. But not where it counts.' She gave me a wink, and I wished I could relate, but all I knew about sex was what I had learnt in books and movies.

'Are you seeing Daniel on the side?' I asked, suppressing my anticipated outrage.

'Daniel? No, he is cute, but there is no — how do you say — cigarette lighter going round?'

'Spark?'

'No spark. And besides, you like him, Naomi.'

'But he doesn't like me.' I was waiting for her to contradict me, to tell me that he had confessed his love for me, that he was working up the courage to tell me, but since he was a chicken she would do it for him. She didn't want us to waste any more time.

'Maybe not in the way you would like. Has he had a girlfriend before? You think he is gay? Look, your glass is empty. Would you like another drink?'

'No, no. I'm not feeling too well. I think I'll take a taxi home.' And I pushed my way out of the booth, through the throng, and onto the street.

'What's wrong, dear?' the taxi driver asked, following my tears down his rear vision mirror.

'I've been sick,' I sobbed. 'My body turned on me.'

'Well, what are you doing out so late? You get an early night. My wife gets a little teary when she's under the weather. Me, I haven't had a sick day in twenty years.' He beamed, and moved on to the foreigners — those Asians and Somalis who were running taxi rackets, and how I wasn't to get in those cabs: they didn't even have their licence, couldn't speak English. I willed my tears to wash him away.

Camilla announced over a bowl of burnt lentils that she was moving out. Pedro Almodóvar's *Women on the Verge of a Nervous Breakdown* was on mute. 'It is your lentils; in Italy they would not do this.'

Daniel rolled his eyes at me; he had been smoking cigarettes and drinking wine with her on the stairs while the lentils boiled dry. I stared at him impassively: I could not forgive him for not loving me.

Camilla had also prepared slices of rich, grainy mozzarella, from a ball wound by an old Italian woman in Island Bay. She layered it with ripe tomatoes and basil and squiggled olive oil across it.

'I found another flat. It is closer to town. No big hill to climb: *ayeee*, my shoes will be spared. The men eat meat, they are computer programmers. I will move in this weekend.'

I reached for another large helping of the mozzarella, storing the taste under my tongue. Daniel looked hurt.

'But what is wrong with this place? We've had lots of fun together.'

'There is mould growing in my bedroom. And I don't like going down the hall, it is spooky. But we can still go to bars together, Daniel. And you too, Naomi. I want to find you a boyfriend before I leave the country.' I cringed, wishing she hadn't winkled out my secret. 'Watch, this bit is so funny!' She scrabbled around for the TV remote and turned up the volume. The hook-nosed fiancé was having an orgasm in her drugged-gazpacho sleep.

Daniel and I gave up the lease after Camilla moved out. I blamed the house for my illness, and now that we weren't going to be an item, I couldn't forgive his stinginess. I moved into a sun-drenched flat in Mt Victoria and absorbed solar rays on the roof like a cat. Daniel found a downtown apartment. His flatmates were a married couple, a lawyer and an accountant, who took heroin holidays in the Vietnamese section of Sydney. They came back with scarred arms, thrashing and shivering in their rooms for days afterwards. Daniel brought them glasses of water and made sure they didn't leave the house until their holiday leave was used up.

We met up at a bar a couple of months later.

'You look good, Naomi!' Camilla kissed me on both cheeks. 'You have got a tan.' But it was more than that. I had kissed my flatmate at a party in the weekend, and when he saw me in the kitchen the next day we kissed again. 'And you, Daniel, you look different too — is there anything you would like to tell us? You found someone to love?'

'Who would have me? I'm quite unlovable.'

Camilla laughed.

'How's your flat going?' I asked her.

'It is wonderful. Did I tell you, I have a new one? Finally, one that I like, with two Maori sisters. The girls took me to stay at their marae. We sang and played guitar and we ate and we drank, we slept together in the meeting house for two nights. I want to be Maori, oh, I want to be Maori!'

'Great,' I said. She wasn't immune to jealousy. 'So how is Hugh?'

''Ugo? He is 'Ugo. He still doesn't like to go out at night. He might come back to Italy with me, but he does not want to teach English again. Did I tell you? I am going back in a month. I will write up my research at home. But you must both come and visit me there!'

'Yes, we'd love to,' Daniel said. 'I want to see the Sistine Chapel and all of the masters' paintings in real life.'

'Well, you must stay with me in my apartment — you must stay for a while. You cannot be a tourist: you will learn the language and find a place of your own. Here, here is my address.' She scribbled on her moleskin notebook and tore off the pieces for us.

'We will,' I said, stowing the paper in my wallet. 'I'll write.' I did not think I would go with Daniel. I imagined my flatmate and me bumping over the cobbled streets on Camilla's Vespa, my arms around his waist. I imagined stopping for an espresso, and drinking it standing up. I imagined dancing in a Latin club with Camilla, then excusing ourselves at 3am to go and make love. I imagined finding an Italian shoe shop that specialised in long, broad feet.

But I never did write to Camilla. And when we had finally saved the money to go to Italy, five years later, the piece of paper had melted like snow.

That's where the
problem lies.
The bok choy is
yellow.

COMING UP ROSES

Imagine that you're a statistic.

Not just a demographic: a white girl living in a white suburb with a white picket fence and a white fridge that you just cleaned with some white Jif.

No, imagine that you are the kind of statistic that people have files on. There's one at Child, Youth and Family. There's one at Work and Income. There's one at the police. You were an orphan, you were a delinquent, you got knocked up at sixteen, you had an abortion, you learnt about condoms, you went professional at eighteen. By the time you turn twenty-two, you've enrolled yourself at university and found a nice flat in Newtown, but it's too late, you're already crazy.

Not *crazy* crazy; not walking through town in your slippers with a cluster of dreadlocks forming at the back of your head, your lipstick applied beyond the circumference of your lips. No, just crazy enough that you don't sleep at night. When you do, you see your mother watering her roses. They bloom from the hole in her head she hasn't noticed yet. Just crazy enough that women powdering their noses on the bus give you panic attacks. Discreet, indiscernible ones, freezing you in your seat four stops past your own. Then you have to walk home, through the rain, through the wind, wondering whether you'll ever be able to breathe normally again.

Your university friends, who are demographics rather than statistics, are almost jealous. You seem exotic. Your black hair and green eyes help. You are fashionably gaunt, and your white skin provokes comparisons to silent film stars. They ask you if you've seen *Sunset Boulevard*. You lie, because although you've seen more ugliness than they have, you haven't watched as many movies. You rent it from the video shop.

Although you haven't revealed much, your university friends are researchers. They piece bits together over coffee. They ask which step triggers the buzzer at the Ghuznee Street brothel. Sometimes at parties, when you're pouring all the dregs of wine bottles into one paper cup, boys who want to be poets put their hands on your shoulder and say, Sofia, you've experienced so much, and I haven't even lived yet. Can you help me? You shrug and ask if they have a cigarette. Once you've held their wrist to steady the flame, you excuse yourself to go to the bathroom and never come back.

Despite your evasiveness, you are looking for true love. And here comes your organic vegetable delivery for the week. You may drink like a fish, smoke like a chimney, take acid like Timothy Leary, but you are conscientious with your greens. No meat, no dairy: only organics, wholegrains and pulses. And lots of bok choy.

That's where the problem lies. The bok choy is yellow. You ring up the organic vegetable delivery boy. You tell him you want a replacement. He tells you you are a part of a co-op, not a capitalist dream. You ask him why he owns a cellphone then. He says it's not so people can ring up and chew his ear off. You tell him it's the simple things in life that matter. Like green bok choy. He tells you to grow your own. You say, look, you fucker, I wouldn't be paying for organic veges if I could grow my own. He says it's easy. He has seedlings. He offers to come around and plant them for you. You say, see you soon, then. You don't think you will.

The organic vegetable delivery boy turns up with seedlings wrapped in damp Chinese newspaper. You invite him inside for a cup of tea. His name is Olaf. He doesn't take soy milk. He relaxes when you roll up a cigarette. Can I have one of those? he asks.

The soil under your kitchen window is hard and you don't have a trowel. You use a kitchen fork. As you are digging around, you hear something go clink. You pull out the fork to find a ring on its prongs. It is encrusted with dirt. Try it on, says Olaf.

First, your middle finger. Your knuckles are too big. Same with your forefinger. Your little finger is too spindly. The only one left is your ring finger.

So does this mean we're engaged? asks Olaf.

Fuck off, you say. You swap it to your right hand. Olaf kisses you. By the time you've got over your shock, your tongue studs have locked.

You and Olaf go on a date. He suggests a Malaysian restaurant on Ghuznee Street, but you don't go to Ghuznee Street any more. You won't explain why. Over dinner in Courtenay Place you break the news to him that the bok choy seedlings have died. Olaf looks angry. What did you do to them? he says. They're special extra-hardy bok choy. My dad gave them to me.

And why would the bok choy your dad gave you be so hardy?

Cause Dad's a plant scientist. He bred them so that even neglectful people could grow them.

You mean they're genetically engineered? you ask.

Olaf shrugs. There aren't any frog genes in them. What the hell did you do to them?

I'm like a walnut tree, you say in your best Gloria Swanson voice. Everything around me dies.

Tell me about it, says Olaf. First there was my cat, Snifter, who was run over by a tractor, and then there were my guinea pigs, which I accidentally blew up with my chemistry set. But plants — I'm good with plants.

You realise Olaf's tattoo has been applied like an apple sticker. Peeled off, he is 100% demographic. You wonder how easily he scares.

You tell him about the Cliff Richard concert.

You always hated Cliff, but your mother loved him. Your mother had been dead for a couple of months and you wanted to do something in her memory, so you bought yourself a ticket. You got quite drunk before the show. There you were, sobbing to 'Living Doll', and you had an idea. You pushed your way up to the front, digging her brass urn out of your backpack. You opened the lid, punctured the plastic bag and swung it around above your head. The ashes sifted across the audience, and over Cliff, sticking to the sweat that cascaded down his forehead. Security kicked you out before you could empty the bag. A good thing, too: your mother had specified she was to be scattered over the roses.

You look at Olaf to see how he has taken it. So far so good. He has resisted the temptation to pat your hand. Blood and bone, he says. Good for the soil.

Olaf comes around with more seedlings. He brings a trowel. He pops in every morning on his delivery run to water them. You admire them when you come home from lectures. They are a vital green.

One day you find a rose bush planted beside the bok choy. You try not to panic, but when you close your eyes you see blood. In the middle of the night you go outside and pour bleach over the roots.

Olaf furrows his brow when first the petals, then the leaves drop off. Are you sure you haven't tried to look after these plants? he asks.

So there it was, true love growing outside your window, and you killed it. How was Olaf to know? You haven't told him how she died. Sometimes your craziness wafts through rooms, like the smell of Sunday roast.

But Olaf is stubborn, maybe a little masochistic. He replaces the rose bush with marigolds. They scare away the caterpillars, he says. He harvests the surviving bok choy and you stand them to attention in the fridge door. The ones that don't fit you wash and halve to stir-fry. You ask Olaf if he'd like to stay for dinner.

You are surprised to awake beside him in the morning. The bleach mustn't have spread as far as you thought. You nudge his shoulder. Have you ever had bok choy for breakfast?

He twists the ring around your finger, polishing the emerald. Can I have toast instead? he asks.

He wishes he were
a botanist.

CROSSING MT TONGARIRO

THE MANGATEPOPO HUTT

'These boots don't fit, Ger. They're too short.'

'You can borrow mine if you want.'

'Don't be stupid. Yours will be two sizes too big. And your feet will be way-squashed if you wear these. Bugger. I should have tried them on at Melanie's before I left.'

'I did tell you, Jen. Do you think you can tramp in them?'

'God, just. My toes are going to get munted, though.'

Gerard sighs. They haven't even started walking.

Jen strides along the track despite her boots, ignoring the orange grass, the white tissue-bud of flower, the red berries that grow out of black lava rock. She habitually rushes towards deadlines. Gerard is left behind, taking pictures that aren't as good as those in his native flora and fauna book. He wishes he were a botanist. His grandfather had a compendium of cuttings, collected for his Honours degree. Each leaf was named in HB pencil, in English, Maori and Latin.

'Gerard, are you coming? We've gotta get over this mountain so we can catch the three o'clock bus on the other side.'

'Jen, it's 8.30. We've got plenty of time.'

Jen snorts through her nose, a mannerism Gerard used to find endearing. Now it pisses him off, along with the blackheads above her lip, and the lists she makes for the supermarket and leaves at home. She's so sour these days, although he grants she has her reasons.

Gerard was relieved when Jen miscarried. Babies were what they *ought* to have, but not what he wanted. Jen had been elated, despite her morning sickness. 'It's no worse than a hangover,' she would say, nibbling on a breakfast water cracker, then puking it over the succulents on the way to work. 'And I've had plenty of experience at those.'

He remembers the day they went to get the nuchal fold test. It was the Wednesday before Easter. Her nausea had faded the previous week, and she'd had her hair dyed to celebrate. She'd been worried that the chemicals would poison the baby, so she'd spent valuable work time on the internet. The results were inconclusive. Her hairdresser painted it copper with red streaks, like mountain tussock.

The radiographer frowned at the ultrasound, and excused herself to find the obstetrician. 'You're right, no heartbeat,' he said to the radiographer, wiping the jelly off Jen's stomach with a paper towel.

'What does that mean?' asked Jen, even though Ger could tell she knew already.

'This way,' said the obstetrician, holding the door open

for them. He left them sitting on office chairs as he murmured in the back corridor with the radiographer. Then he came through, waving a printout in his hand. The foetus had died the week before.

'Was it my hair?' Jen asked.

The obstetrician looked at her quizzically. 'Interesting,' he said. He assumed a sympathetic expression. 'Anything may have triggered it. Most often it's nature's way of deleting its mistakes. It probably had a congenital abnormality. We'll book you in for a D & C since it hasn't spontaneously aborted.' He looked back at Jen's head. 'Who's your hairdresser?'

Gerard drove home, furious on Jen's behalf, slapping the steering wheel and honking at minor transgressions. 'Could you believe that guy? So insensitive. Deleting a mistake? That was our fucking baby he was talking about.'

Jen wasn't listening. 'I told everyone at work. Mum said I should wait until twelve weeks but I couldn't. I told my clients. What am I going to say tomorrow? They ask me about the baby before they ask about their job.' She pressed her fingers into the place where the embryo floated inside its bean skin. She asked Gerard to stop at The Warehouse. He waited outside in the car, yelling along to his most hard-core CD. Jen returned with a sack of Easter eggs.

'I'll put one on everyone's desk early tomorrow morning.'

'Why?'

'Good for office morale.'

The hoarse sobs came on Good Friday. The living room was a mess of tissues, empty red wine bottles and full ashtrays. Gerard dragged her off the sofa Saturday afternoon, down to their favourite bar. They were evicted at 11.30pm for Easter Sunday closing.

THE SODA SPRINGS

They've got to the steep part of the climb. The part where clefts of boulders seize ankles and twist. Where boots rub toes into bubble-wrap blisters. The part where lungs strain and bulge, where you wish you had crampons, a walking stick, anything. Jen's the first to break.

'Fuck this climb. You didn't tell me it was going to be so hard.'

'It's a mountain, Jen. What did you expect?'

'What is this mountain-climbing bullshit anyway? Just because you've climbed it doesn't mean you've conquered nature or anything.'

'Look at the view. Look at it.'

'It's better from a plane. From a ski-lift, for Christ's sake.'

'Please, Jen. It's beautiful up there. I promise.'

'You promise so much, Ger.'

Gerard bites his lip. It's true he's still in the same crappy call-centre job even though he said he'd find another one. Media studies had seemed like such a good option at the time. It's true that they haven't had much sex since Jen got pregnant, and that was six months ago. He doesn't know why. It's just — well, things are different now. The butterflies that flitted when he looked at her laid their eggs and died. The caterpillars are chewing through his cabbage bloom of love.

When Jen was pregnant she surrounded herself with baby books. She rolled whispery names around her tongue. Florence Hannah Emily Winona Mary-Lou Beatrice. Jack Jonty Michael Patrick Llewellyn. The books are still there. No longer on her bedside table but in her underpants drawer, along with the orange and red pixie bonnet she tried to knit.

She's doing it again. That whispering thing. Each boulder she climbs, it becomes more persistent. But it's not baby names she's saying — the fs are scud missiles, the ks burst out like letter-bombs. Gerard puts his hand on her shoulder but she slaps it away.

SOUTH CRATER

They eat chocolate when they get to the top, settling into a companionable silence. He hopes she'll like the next part of the walk, across a pockmarked moonscape. He remembers coming up here with his grandmother when he was twelve and she was seventy-two. He had marvelled at her muscular calves, surely stolen from a sleeping thirty-year-old who now needed two walking sticks. When he first saw the crater, it only took a squint to summon the spaceship. *One small step for man . . .* He remembers trying to leap, surprised by the gravity that pulled him down. Gran laughed and handed him another egg sandwich.

When Gran died last year, aged ninety, Jen had been supportive for a week. She'd come to Gran's funeral, she'd sat in the front row beside him. But she couldn't understand why Gerard was slumped in front of the telly two weeks later, shunning an invitation to a beer tasting. 'Come on, Ger, how long are you going to be a misery-sacks for? She had a good innings. It's time to start living again.'

Jen had mourned efficiently for her own Nana, who counted $5 worth of coins out of her purse each Christmas. Nana petitioned Jen to bank it, but one year she bought tom-bowlers instead. It wasn't her fault Nana broke her hip rolling on an escaped marble. But Nana liked to recount Jen's assassination attempt whenever her hip twinged. Jen's protestations spurred her on. It was Nana's favourite story until she forgot everything she knew.

When Gerard, Jen and Gran had their first card game together, Gran pulled Ger into the kitchen to help load the trolley with club sandwiches and drinks. 'I don't know about this one, Gerry. She's too knowing. Why don't you find someone younger? A sweet girl who'll look after you.'

He laughed. 'Like you, Gran? I'm in love. Like you were, with Grandad.'

Gran misted up at the reminder of Harold. 'He was so handsome when he was concentrating on his drawings.' She'd reluctantly given Ger her blessing. 'Just be careful,' she said as she pulled the brandy decanter out of the cupboard.

'Why did your Gran accuse me of cheating?' Jen asked Ger as they walked home. 'Doesn't she like me?'

'Course she likes you. It's part of the game; she doesn't like to lose.'

'How come you spend so much time with an old lady?'

'Gran's great. She drove an ambulance in London during the war.'

'Oh, that's cool,' she'd said uncertainly.

THE EMERALD LAKES

Jen doesn't say much in the South Crater. But when they slide down the scree to the Emerald Lakes he hears an intake of breath.

'Quite something, eh?'

'What an amazing colour. It's like going to see the Wizard of Oz. I'm Dorothy and you're the Tin Man.'

Gerard wonders whether he's the Cowardly Lion instead. He opens up his backpack. He pulls out the pieces of jam on toast that he stole from the hotel breakfast buffet. 'You hungry?'

Jen nods and takes the toast. Up here everything tastes good.

'Jen,' says Gerard as he takes a squashed kiwifruit out of the bottom of his bag, 'do you still love me?'

'Of course I still love you,' she says, but it's automatic and Gerard wonders whether she means it. 'Do you still love me, Ger?'

'Yeah, I do,' he says.

THE KETETAHI HOT SPRINGS

Jen's mood lifts when she realises it's downhill. Gerard doesn't mention the bashed toes and aching calves that come with the descent. Instead he admires the plants, dwarfed by altitude. The further down they go, the taller the plants get, and Gerard has the sensation that he and Jen are shrinking, their legs worn down from walking. It's a pity you can't bathe in the hot springs any more. He remembers sitting in the murky water with Gran, laughing as the skirt on her pineapple-print bathing suit bobbed on the surface. Jen would have enjoyed the muscle relief. They could have had fun together. The way his nose feels at the moment, he doesn't know whether he is going to sneeze or cry.

THE GRAND CHATEAU

Gerard and Jen sit in the hotel lobby, drinking red wine. Above them hangs an enormous oil painting of the Pink and White Terraces. They look like coconut ice, and Gerard wonders whether a British colonist ever tried to slice some off with his penknife.

'How do you feel, Jen?' he asks.

'I'm so tired. I think I might have lost a couple of toenails. I'm glad I did it, though.'

'Yeah, I'm glad too.'

'You know, Ger, I took my temperature this morning.'

'Did you?'

'Yeah. And I'm ovulating.'

'Great.' Gerald shifts slightly.

'Why did you do that?'

'What?'

'Why did you move your leg away? Don't you want to do it?'

'Course I do, Jen. What do you take me for?'

'Someone with a testosterone deficiency, unless he's in a pair of hiking boots. Hey, you can keep your boots on if you like.' Jen smiles, like she used to.

Gerard feels something stir. 'I brought condoms, Jen. You know, so we could just . . . '

'Why did you bring condoms? I hate condoms. We don't need them any more.'

'I've been having second thoughts.'

'You can't have second thoughts now. We decided, Ger. This is what we're going to do next. For once in our five years together we've made a decision.'

'Have we? Did we both make this decision? Or did you make this decision?'

'Somebody had to. Look at you, floating along at the call centre, Mr Going-Nowhere-Fast. Always saying you want to be a botanist. But have you enrolled for that course yet? You've done nothing, Ger, except use up the lunch paper to press your leaves.'

'What's wrong with the call centre? Pays my bills, gives me time to think about stuff. Not like you, Jen, and your hot-shot marketing job. You think of this pregnancy as another one of your projects, with deadlines and strategic outcomes. Once you've given birth you're going to cross it off your to-do list. Who's going to look after the kid, Jen? I bet you're assuming me, since I'm such a lousy breadwinner. When are you going to inform me about part two of the project?'

Jen says nothing. She gulps her wine. The pianist plays 'Auld Lang Syne' even though it's September, and the two billiards players sing along.

'We could share the childcare.'

'Maybe I don't want to share the childcare. Maybe I've already downloaded the enrolment papers. Maybe I'm not the dad type.'

'What would you have done if the baby hadn't died? Left me in labour?'

'I would have stuck it out . . . but it might not have been great, Jen. We would have been one of those families that stay together for the sake of the kids.'

'Hold on, are you saying that you don't want to be

together any more?'

Gerard stops. He didn't think he wanted to break up, but it seems like the only way out.

'Fuck. Fuck. I'm thirty-four. Just my fucking luck. Have you seen the statistics? I'm the worst demographic to find a mate; my fertility is plummeting. Why couldn't you have left me when I still had a chance?'

'I love you, Jen.'

'No you don't. You're just saying that.' Jen stands up, shoving her cellphone and wallet into her daypack. She fishes the car keys out of the front pocket and walks out of the lobby, leaving her boots by the sofa where she unlaced them.

'Jen, don't go. It's too late. You're tired. Stay; you've paid for the room.'

Jen hobbles over the gravel drive in her thick wool socks. She climbs into the SUV (Jen's company car; he's always giving her shit about its environmental footprint) and hits reverse, fast enough to blast Gerard off his feet. He watches her from his arse, the sharp stones digging into the palms of his hands.

ROOM 313

Gerard lies on the hotel bed, flicking through the channels on the 24-inch TV. He ordered room service because he hates looking like a sad fuck eating alone in a restaurant. Besides, he's too drunk to dress for dinner. They delivered the venison and chocolate mousse along with the boots Jen left in the lobby. He's impressed with their detective work. The boots stand next to his, as if Jen's popped out for a cigarette.

The plates are on the floor, dripping their juices onto the carpet. At least something will stain them, if it's not going to be sex. He rolls off the bed and grabs another mini bottle of spirits from the fridge. He looks through the window at Mt Tongariro, indigo in the dusk. It was so beautiful when he crossed it with his grandmother. He wishes Jen could have seen it the same way.

Through her wall,
you could hear
her rattle

POD

Do you mind that your grandmother is not your grandmother? That she died before you'd been thought of, before your mother met your father at a party in Ihaka Street, when she still had long hair and wore mini-dresses, and he still rode a motorbike?

Do you mind that her replacement is called Pip — not Grandma, but what you spit from a mandarin? Do you mind that she thinks you are spoilt, that every Cuisenaire rod, every Fisher Price xylophone is a proof of that?

You don't mind now. Now you are sitting on the scratchy sofa watching *Coronation Street* and eating home-bottled peaches with cream and cornflakes. Your bowl sits on a mini-table with cabriole legs, topped by a claret-coloured placemat and a table napkin with a silver ring. Your grandfather eats the same, and your mother says that Pip looks after Grandpa very well, always has. She'd been his best secretary.

Tonight you will be sleeping in the blue room. The blue

room is where Pip puts the baskets of pot pourri that her stepchildren give her. The pink room is where Pip puts the presents she gives to her stepchildren, signing their cards 'Love, Dad.' You know this because the last time you stayed, you rummaged through its bureau. In the top drawer there were soaps and bottles of Yardley perfume, handkerchiefs and books on gardening. In the middle drawer there were lavender sachets and boxes of chocolate almonds. In the bottom drawer there were argyle socks and crystal ashtrays, bottles of Old Spice aftershave and tins of fork-marked shortbread.

You prefer the pink room. It has two beds and a basin, so you don't have to go to the bathroom to brush your teeth or get a glass of water. The cupboard is filled with fur coats, and if you pushed through them you would feel pine needles pricking your flesh, the crunch of ice beneath your blue roman sandals. You couldn't eat the Turkish delight because you would turn to stone.

In the blue room there is one bed, which Pip will turn down for you, slipping a hottie in a knitted mustard jersey between the sheets. She will leave a glass of milk and a chocolate digestive on your bedside table. In the blue room there is a photograph of your mother and your aunt as children. They wear tartan kilts and white jerseys, cable-knitted by your real grandmother. Now they look like puffy cartoons of themselves.

You wonder whether you will still be you when you grow up. Earlier, you clomped around in Pip's Cuban heels, pink lipstick smeared across your lips and cheeks. You tried on her pearls, opening up her jewellery box to unbend the ballerina. Pip told you off when she found you, so you went to the orchard and ate until your tummy hurt. You lay on your bed in the blue room and waited for the stones in your belly to shoot root tendrils down your legs, for the green leaves to sprout from your pores, plums dripping off your fingertips.

Mrs Ford is sleeping in the pink room. She is Pip's mother, a widow. She is shaky and delicate and broke her hip on the path outside her council flat. Pip brings her soup to slide down her throat, pinched as a twist on a brown paper bag. Through the wall, you hear her rattle like a dried flax pod. In the morning, as the magpies quardle-ardle on the curving drive, you watch her eating little black pills. You think they are seeds that have burst from her in the middle of the night.

Pip worries more about Mrs Ford than about you. She worries over a stockpot. She drops a chicken skeleton into it. You lick its steam off the windows but it doesn't taste how it smells. A bell rings. In the kitchen the servants' light box says it's from the pink room. Pip removes stones from stewed apricots. She puts the bowl on a tray.

Mrs Ford shivers in the sunroom, a blanket over her knees. Your grandfather carried her through in his Christmas-ham arms. Spit hangs from her lip like chandelier glass. Pip reads to her from the *Woman's Weekly*. Princess Diana has just got married. She had a train as long as a cul-de-sac. Pip puts the crossword on Mrs Ford's lap and fills in the squares for her. Mrs Ford grunts when she gets it wrong, and Pip rubs out the pencil. You wonder how somebody could love someone when they are so old.

They don't notice when you slip out to the pool. It is past the tennis court, through the bush. Pip says there are no foxes in New Zealand, but there are foxes in the trees, there are snaky worms in the hollows.

The pool is empty, but if it were full it might freeze over so that girls in silver skates could cut figure-of-eights into it. The ice might trap green frogs and violets. Your mother used to swim here when her mother was alive. She wore a blue and red bikini, and sipped fruit punch with the boyfriends she had before your father.

You walk across the bottom, kicking rotten leaves. You call and your voice bounces back to you. You put your ear to the cracks in the concrete to find words that might have caught there. You call again. But this time it is Pip who echoes you.

You lie on the bed in the blue room. You are not allowed to come out until morning.

You close your eyes and listen to Mrs Ford rattle. She is louder than a flax pod tonight; she sounds like the engine of an old car.

Mrs Ford sits behind the wheel of Princess Diana's wedding car, the top pushed down. She wears a white dress and her train snows on the street behind her. 'Would you like some Turkish delight?' she asks.

'No,' you say. But she is shaking the box, and it is too delicious to refuse. You eat until you are dusted in icing sugar. You are a spoilt girl.

When you open your eyes the rattle has stopped. You wriggle your fingers to check you are not made of stone. The candlewick bedspread moves. You sit up, swinging your legs to the floor. You are happy because you are still you. You put on your slippers and open your door. The door to the pink room is closed. Black seeds spill out onto the hall carpet. 'Pip?' you call.

There is no porridge in the kitchen. There is no cream.

POD

Your grandmother who is not your grandmother sits at the table with her face in her hands.

'Where is Mrs Ford?' you ask. She doesn't answer.

Your mother comes as the doctor leaves. She wasn't meant to collect you so soon. 'It's only Tuesday,' you say, hoping she will explain. She pulls you close to her.

'Let me know if you need help with the arrangements,' she says, touching Pip's shoulder. Pip flinches. 'Or with Dad's work.'

'We'll manage. I've done this before.'

'But last time it wasn't your mother.'

Pip looks up. Her face is swollen; she looks scared. 'No,' she says. 'It wasn't.'

Zach has had progressively smaller girlfriends, as though he's playing a weird game of Russian dolls.

Just Married

1. Christina's driving home from church, a stringy Christian folksong stuck in her head. Sometimes she wishes she was Pentecostal rather than Catholic — then there'd be gospel singers or rock groups rather than nuns on flutes and guitar. The congregation is so insipid that if she raises her voice above a whisper they turn to look. Her vocal training hasn't taught her how to sing quietly. 'Use your diaphragm to send your voice to the back of the hall,' her singing teacher would say. 'Come to the water,' she sings. The phrase bounces off the windshield and rings in her ears.

She sees a man standing on the side of the road, his thumb extended. He's not tattooed; he isn't in prison denims. She likes the way his shirt hangs off his broad shoulders, how his hair flops in his eye. The sermon today was about the Good Samaritan. She pushes the brake, indicates, pulls over. She winds down her window. The man limps towards her.

'Thanks for stopping. You don't know how many cars have gone past.'

'No problem. Where are you heading?'

'I'm going to the gym on Broadway. I normally run there, but I hurt my ankle rock-climbing last night.'

'Should you be going at all?'

'I'll just do upper body. Besides, you meet interesting people hitchhiking. I'm Zach, by the way.' He stretches out his hand.

2. To: Lesley Greer <lesleyg@petersoninsurance.co.nz>
From: Zach <zichzach@gmail.com>
Subject: re: congratulations

Yes it's true. How did you hear? I know it's fast but Christina's a Catholic and said she couldn't you know before we married. I grew a kick-ass Magnum PI moustache and after the ceremony we went to a Korean restaurant and sang karaoke. My parents were pretty wild when they found out but not as wild as Christina's. How's your love life? :-)

Zach

3. I almost choke on my chocolate chip biscuit when I read this. Zach dumped me via email; it's ironic that I hear he's married this way as well. The crazy thing is, I didn't know he got hitched. I was just bored on a Friday afternoon, shooting my fingers off. I think about all the things I have been told via email:

1. I'm gay.

2. I've become a Buddhist and am giving up all my worldly possessions, so would you like to buy my electric breadmaker for $50?

3. I had a miscarriage and I think I flushed the foetus.

Don't people believe in phoning any more? I suppose when phones first came out, everyone complained. Before phones, people would traipse through hailstorms, land-slides and thorn bushes to share news. They would cry and hold hands over bowls of turnip soup. Modern news is misspelled, txtd, and deleted once read.

I forward this one to my mates. You can't launch straight into spreadsheets without a little Monday morning soap opera. I expect to field oh-my-god, what, is-he-crazy? responses. I search for a photo of Christina on Zach's Flickr account. It is vital that my friends assure me that I'm prettier than her, although I'm sure they won't be able to tell me that I'm smaller. I hit a perfect six foot. Ever since me, Zach has had progressively more petite girlfriends, as though he's playing a weird game of Russian dolls. Start twisting, split us open, then pull out a more diminutive version. The one after me was five foot nine, then five foot seven, then five foot six. I wonder whether Christina is the solid wooden one in the centre.

4. Zach wakes up in his marital bed, made with wedding-present satin sheets. He likes their slithery skin but he's scared of slipping out of bed.

Christina turns, her cheek crumpled where she fused with the pillow. He brushes a strand of hair away from her face. The dark fuzz above her lip troubles him. He pushes away the mental image of shaving together in front of the mirror. She is his beautiful bride. His bride who wore a Cinderella wedding dress. And he rented a *Saturday Night Fever* white vest to match, but he wasn't sure whether Christina shared the irony. She tutted over the kimchi he spilt down it, and doused it in soda water.

It's Sunday morning and Christina will probably go to Mass. He was surprised when he discovered she was religious, but he wanted to know whether it was true about Catholic girls. No one he knows goes to church any more. He was disturbed at how readily he had bailed from previous relationships, and he thought that marriage might reverse this pattern.

It was novel waiting for sex, and they made up for lost time. But this week it's slipped back to every other night, and they're only six weeks in.

If he cooks Lesley's deluxe pancakes with fresh fruit and cream, will Christina decide to skip church? Will she trade confession for consummation? He slips out of bed and pads to the kitchen. He opens the fridge and takes out eggs and milk. He identifies each tendon that surfaces in his arm, whisking with his Leatherman. He puts flour, baking powder, sugar and salt into another bowl. He make a well in the centre and pours in the liquid. He stirs it, but not too much because he doesn't want to activate the gluten force-field.

He pours the first pancake into a Starship Enterprise shape, but burns it. The rest are perfect. He embellishes them with blueberries and maple syrup, and puts the plates on a tray alongside the coffees.

He blows on Christina's cheek and she opens her eyes. 'Mmmm?'

'Pancakes.'

'Mmm.' She pulls the pillow over her head.

'Come on, Christina, I made them especially.' Other girls have sat up and gobbled them, arranging their phone numbers on his fridge with alphabet magnets.

'I don't eat in the morning.'

Then what has she done with the toast he buttered her? Fed the ducks?

Christina picks a blueberry eye off the pancake Mr Spock. She glances at the alarm clock. 'Oh no, I'm going to be late!' She pushes the tray aside.

'Don't go, Christina. Stay in bed with me.'

'Not now, Zach.'

He sighs. He picks up the pancake and eats it, one ear at a time.

5. Christina's having second thoughts. Now's not such a good time since they're already married. She was suspiciously qualm-free as she zipped up the Costume Cave wedding dress. Sometimes she's surfing the wave of preordination, other times it rips her under. When Zach first shook her hand through the wound-down window they both got an electric shock. Zap: this is the one. But perhaps it was a warning. This is not your fate. Lock your doors, accelerate.

Christina is often palsied by fate. She's driving along and she thinks, if I go down Ribber Street, will my whole life change? Will I stop to help a woman changing her tyre and discover she's the next Mother Theresa? Will I be so inspired that I will go and live in Bolivia to feed the poor? Or what if I go down Sullivan Street — will I find a kitten, and knock on my future husband's door in search of its owner? What if I stop at the service station and miss all these things, my destiny unrealised because I felt like gum?

Christina walks into the cool, dark church, blessing herself with holy water. The sun scatters stained-glass stories across bald pates and polished wood. She genuflects, even though Vatican II said you didn't have to. She sits on the hard seats as the flautist warms her pipe with spittle. She turns to page twenty-two of the hymnal.

Is this the silence between the overture and the first movement of love? Or did she agree to something she shouldn't have? If so, she blames her adolescent explorations. *Will you marry me?* she whispered to herself after lights out, scalloped elastic indenting her wrist, her two fingers pulsing the new-found place. *Yes. Yes, yes, yes.*

She doesn't really know Zach yet. She's not interested in rock climbing or eighties television shows. He does say he'll help her make music. She's sick of singing to the vacuum cleaner, to the shower-head, to the congregation who disapprove of show-offs. Zach has a new computer with software that can loop her voice, that can layer it with beats and burn it onto CD. He's just got to figure out how to use it. Maybe this is the divine plan. Besides, what did her parents have in common?

6. The bitch is prettier than me. My mates say don't be silly, Christina looks like a toilet-paper doll in her wedding dress, and why the hurry, was she pregnant? But she's skinnier, her skin is clearer, and her hair is black, not dirty blonde and in a manky ponytail.

I'm over Zach — don't get me wrong. He was my first boyfriend, my first true love, with whom I talked all night and named my imaginary children and learned how to give blow-jobs and fought and broke plates and went on camping trips where I couldn't break the plates because they were made of tin. We exhausted each other. The annoying thing is that since me he has had a progression of true loves and I've only got a profile on an online dating service. Now he's married, and I don't even have a crush, unless you count that flutter I get when the photocopier repairman bends over the machine.

I check out the train timetables on the internet: I might visit. I'm not causing trouble; Zach prides himself on being friends with his exes. What have I got on this weekend? A night out with the usual suspects, pick-and-mixing one another's ex-boyfriends, whose sexual deficiencies we've already been briefed on. It sucks when your own are reported back to you.

7. To: Lesley Greer <lesleyg@petersoninsurance.co.nz>
From: Zach <zichzach@gmail.com>
Subject: re: re: congratulations
Choice! We should go kayaking to that café in the middle of nowhere, for old time's sake. Christina isn't big on outdoor stuff so maybe you could egg her on. Not sure how much you guys have in common but she's a Catholic like you LOL :-p

8. Christina's breathing deep breaths, trying not to yell at Zach for letting his ex-girlfriend stay, the weekend he promised he'd figure out that software. Now he says they're going kayaking, even though she told him she's scared of rivers with their slimy eels. Zach assures her that his ex means nothing to him any more. They're mates; their passion fizzled a year before they broke up. Then why is this ex staking her out?

Christina and Zach wait outside the train station. 'Taxi, taxi, taxi?' ask the men in cheap suits. They sound like cicadas. People wander past, travel-stale, chip-greasy. Zach squints, then waves. 'Lesley! Over here!'

Christina watches her approach. Very tall, with brown skin and broad shoulders. An Amazon. Christina feels puny in comparison.

Zach gives Lesley a hug. Christina surges forward, her hand outstretched. She should have said no. She can't stay, it's too soon. She knows you better than I do. Christina thinks of the cake she baked last night. It was high and round when she took it out of the oven, but the next time she looked it had collapsed. Zach rescued it from the bin, saying it was nothing cream and jam couldn't fix. But Zach said Lesley was good at baking: she had wanted her to admire Christina's afternoon tea.

9. I'm slicing through the water, but Christina's paddle is skidding across the top. Zach circles her, saying encouraging things. She's looking pissed off.

The river is the colour of greenstone. Sometimes I see a glint of silver, maybe a trout, or a lost fork. I haven't kayaked since our last summer together in the Sounds. Zach was irritatingly delighted by the seals. Like a boy. Each time he saw one he would yelp.

Why didn't I try harder? He was keen, even though I was too tired. Then I wouldn't have to consider Trevor from Accounts, who says, 'You might want to cross out your lingerie purchases before you hand me your Visa bill, or I'll get excited.'

But Zach's a pain in the arse. Has taken his top off not because it's too hot. Still doesn't drive. I wonder whether Christina will fatten him up. Not likely — she looks like she forgets to eat. Maybe she's transferred her appetite elsewhere. Maybe she has multiple orgasms.

When our sex life dried up, Zach and I still had great brunches. We'd even talk: none of this swapping newspaper sections. God, I'm starved. I wonder how far away this café is.

10. Zach has pulled ahead, like MacGyver leading the distressed damsels away from the chemical spill. Only Lesley's not distressed. He wonders whether he should stop at an inlet, show them how he can make a flat stone skip seven times. But would that impress Christina?

He knows what he ought to have done this weekend. He ought to have told Lesley to bugger off; he ought to have opened up that GarageBand package. But by the end of the week he's over computers; he wants to be at one with nature. Climbing mountains and cutting vines with his knife. Having sex in the long grass.

Someone walked past when he did that with Lesley. They were a metre away; he heard their voices but kept on going. It's got to be the highlight — no, it's going to be more spectacular with Christina. His beautiful bride. The veil may have been cheesy, but perfect for a TV camera close-up. When they kissed, Christina tasted like a PK advertisement. She made his lips red, and it suited him. Even MacGyver went to Hair & Makeup before a shoot.

Zach turns to wave. The first and the last. Christina's quite a way behind. Lesley waves back. Is Christina doing the fingers?

11. Christina tries to say a Hail Mary, something calming and meditative, but she finds herself cursing instead. Damn, she says as her left paddle hits

the water. Shit, she says, as her right one goes down. She has a blister and her arm feels like it's going to fall off. 'Zach!' she yells.

'Almost there,' he yells back.

No, you bastard, she thinks. Tow me. Put your show-off upper-body strength to some use.

He's right. There it is. A little wooden café on stilts, among the ponga trees and ginger plants. Their scarlet blooms complement the chipped green paint. Christina glides to the pebbly shore and tries to wriggle out, but she tips and falls into a face full of rocks. She struggles, legs a-tangle, ankles caught in the rim, the river claiming the paddle, then the canoe. Zach wades past her to catch them. 'What about me?' she yells. Why don't you stop me from slipping away?

Zach returns to Christina, but it's too late. She's sitting on the river bed, slapping at the eels that may or may not be shimmying up her shirt; she's passing stone-sized sobs. 'Come to the water, you who are thirsty,' she sings, and then begins to laugh. She lies back, baptizes herself, still singing, her voice popping with each bubble that hits the surface. She feels two hands yanking her wrists, and Zach yelling, 'Christina! For God's sake, pull yourself together.'

'What do you mean, *for God's sake*? You don't believe in him. It's for your sake, sweetheart.' She stumbles onto the shore, water running from her shorts, her T-shirt clinging to her. Her nipples are sticking out and she covers them with her hands.

'Are you all right?' Lesley calls.

12. Christina lost the plot! Christina lost the plot! This is fantastic email material.

13. Zach's embarrassed. His wife singing church songs to a balcony of people eating muffins and drinking coffee. Why did he think Catholicism was a turn-on? And how can someone be so un-outdoorsy? He catches Lesley's eye and she ducks behind a ginger plant, bursting with laughter. He can hardly expect her to share his pain.

The café owner rushes out with a towel and a Sleepy River Café T-shirt in plastic wrap (does this happen often?) and bustles Christina inside. Zach follows Lesley as if he's with her and Christina's some hapless tourist.

Lesley orders a chocolate chip muffin and a coffee. Zach chooses a cheese pinwheel and a beer. Lesley changes her order. 'Does chocolate go with beer?' she asks.

'Of course it does,' he says. 'All things bad for you go together.'

'So are you saying that you'd eat a chocolate-steak sandwich?'

'Steak's not bad for you, is it?'

'It doesn't look so bad for you,' says Lesley, her teeth bright in her broad smile.

Is she flirting? He summons spreadsheets and blocked toilets. He hopes Christina doesn't reappear soon. 'How often do normal couples have sex?' he asks, even though he shouldn't. But Lesley has a degree in psychology, and she reads those kinds of magazines.

Finger on chin, Dr Lesley appears. 'Depends on whether you're Scandinavian. Or married. Whether you're on Prozac. If you've got kids. Then you're really screwed. Or not.'

'So how often do those people do it?'

'Once a month . . . a couple of times a year.'

'Oh my god. Remind me never to have kids.'

'Surely that's on the top of Christina's agenda.'

'We haven't even mentioned it yet. Too busy, you know . . . ' Because it's important that Lesley realises how justified Zach was in dismissing her.

Christina comes out of the bathroom, leaving a trail of drips on the shiny black floor. The T-shirt reaches her knees. She could fit inside Lesley, and that image makes him so excited he has to drop a serviette on his lap and lean forward to eat his pinwheel.

Christina sits down. 'Are you going to order anything?' he asks.

'I'm not hungry.'

'What do you mean you're not hungry?'

'I want to go home.'

'You can't go home. You've got to canoe back.'

'No I don't. The café owner said they pick the one-way kayaks up in a trailer. And I can hitch a lift into town with her son. Lesley can drive you, can't she?'

'Yep,' says Lesley, that smirk returning.

'Christina, can't you try a little harder? Can't you do this for me?'

'I think I've done my bit, Zach. It's your turn now.'

The café owner is calling and pointing. Her son stands in the door, his white-boy afro back-lit.

Zach stands and kisses her passionately, but it's for Lesley's sake really. Christina doesn't yield. She walks away, steam outlines of her small feet evaporating behind her.

The wooden roller-blind
flew up to reveal a
giant aluminium teapot

FALLING

I got a crush on the first boy who paid me any attention. He rode his bicycle across my path as I was walking home. 'I've seen you,' he said, 'at church. What are you doing this afternoon?'

Did he want to have sex? The thought filled me with revulsion and excitement. He was blond; I didn't like blond hair. His skin was tanned, egg-speckled, undulated with muscle. His legs were tumescent in his pink and black bicycle shorts.

'Um, I've got stuff to do,' I said, and hurried over the road.

'See ya,' he called after me.

I didn't do homework or practise my bassoon. I lay on my bed and fizzed. A boy wanted to hang out with me. *Me.* My body chattered. The scene played over in my head, and in each take his hair became more like precious metal. By dinnertime I was unable to eat or sit still.

I didn't absorb anything at school the next week.

My bassoon teacher sent me back to class halfway through my lesson. I shredded the insides of my cheeks. Boys were a rare commodity at a girls' school.

The classroom was afflicted by an Indian summer, and we sweated Rorschach blots at our armpits and breasts. No amount of opening louvre windows or fanning with exercise books released the stink. I found out that his name was Kevin. After lights out I imagined sitting on his crossbar, his hands either side of me. He would ride us towards the river, tipping over when blinded by the sunshine. We would fall onto a knoll of grass and roll, one on top of the other.

Kevin appeared just as I was about to refuse to go to church any more. Church was boring. I did believe in God, but if I could find someone to have sex with, I would definitely use birth control. I was selfish during Prayers of the Faithful, rarely tacking requests for disarmament onto my standard order for boyfriends and maths test passes.

Now I prepared for Mass with a new zeal. I ironed my clothes, I washed my hair. I applied stage makeup that my mother called tarty but was designed so that Kevin would think my eyes were big across the room. When it was Communion I stood in line behind him. I trailed his fine blond hairs from his nape to his collar. When Kevin turned from the priest, working the Body of Christ off the roof of his mouth with his tongue, I looked at him. If he looked back, the aftershocks tremored for hours.

Church had improved in other ways. Father Gregory Payne had recently joined the parish. He drove a yellow convertible and had shoulder-length black hair that fell in ringlets. Was it a permanent wave? He glided up the aisle in his robes, carrying the sceptre, but once he was up the stairs he swaggered. The pulpit couldn't contain him. He zigzagged past the altar and down the stairs again; he hollered his sermon.

People whispered over their presbytery cups of tea. Was he refreshing or was he cocky? Why did a hip guy like him decide to become a priest? A husk to contain the love of the Lord he was not. I had seen him with a bucket of fried chicken, the grease shining his chin. There were burnt rubber marks on the church drive. The whisperers mentioned certain women who invited him to dinner when their husbands were away.

I was to get confirmed that year. I had already been christened, and had dressed like a mini-bride for my First Communion. If I wanted a full Nuptial Mass (I wasn't sure if I had the patience for it, but my future mother-in-law might insist), I had to complete my initiation. My mother was surprised I agreed so easily: I signed my name beneath Kevin W. Abernathy's.

Abernathy. According to the phone book, he lived on Fergusson Street. I perused his house. I watched his mother feed his strawberry-blonde sister mashed pumpkin. I pulled the daisies off her bush to statistically analyse whether he loved me or not.

A friend, Ali, had a cousin who went to Kevin's Catholic school, and over a stack of after-school toast she reported that he wasn't that bright. 'Neither's my cousin,' she said, her mouth full of peanut butter. 'Let's ring him and find out.'

'Don't be stupid.' I put mugs of milk in the microwave

and watched them circle, wondering if it was true your retinas could melt this way. I spooned instant coffee into them. When I turned around the phone book was open and Ali had dialed the number.

'Hi Kevin. Katy really likes you.'

'No, no!' I howled, jamming a mug down on the disconnect button. Did he know who Katy was? I redialled to say it wasn't true.

'Hi, Katy,' he said.

I hung up.

Our confirmation classes were to be taken by Father Greg. We were dropped off by our parents after dinner, and Father Greg ushered us into the presbytery living room. He sighed into his black leather sofa, kicking off Italian tasselled loafers. A black cat spiked its back. 'This is Panther,' he told us.

I called the cat by twiddling my fingers. My neck was sore from sneaking looks at Kevin. Our eyes kept clanging. Panther climbed onto me, a balm for embarrassment. He punctured my thighs with his claws and settled into a purring oval. Father Greg was talking about Love, but all I could feel was damp. Was I getting my period? No, the cat was dribbling. She yowled as I pushed her from my lap, snagging my tights on her way down.

'Sorry, mate, she's got a few tooth issues,' Father Greg said, pointing at the soaked patch on my skirt.

Everyone laughed, except for Esperanza, the Goth. She was fingering a crucifix that had hung on the wall at the beginning of the session.

After our session we were invited down to the lounge. The wooden roller-blind to hide the kitchen counter flew up, to reveal a giant aluminium teapot and plates of biscuits. 'Pass them around, will you, Kevin?' said Father Greg.

'Hands off my gingernut,' Kevin joked as I reached for one.

I froze.

'Nah, take one,' he said. 'Looks like you need it.' He smiled at my stain. I reached forward abruptly, scattering the biscuits off the plate.

'Shit,' I said.

Kevin knelt down beside me. 'Takes eight seconds for germs to stick.' He shoved a few biscuits in his mouth.

I bit down hard on a biscuit, but it didn't break. Kevin ejected his, two damp computer disks.

'You need to dunk them in tea,' he said.

Father Greg pinged his cup with his signet ring. 'Next on the agenda, we're gonna burn off for a retreat. Get out of our familiar environment so we can focus on the Word. Grab a permission slip, kids, and get your olds to sign it.'

Father Greg waggled the papers, and we plucked them like feathers from a chicken's bum. It said we were going to Castlepoint. We were leaving Friday afternoon, and returning on Sunday.

The road was winding, and I felt carsick. I hated travelling. I just wanted to be there. If Kevin had been assigned to the same car, then maybe my nervous energy would have turbo-charged the engine, but as it was, he was in the minibus with the surfboards. I was in a pale blue Triumph with Bridget and Bernadette, girls from the Catholic school. Bridget's mum was driving. Bridget and Bernadette gossiped about teachers and kids that I didn't know, but not about Kevin. I snapped the ashtray open and shut until Bridget's mum told me to stop.

We drove down the main road to Castlepoint as dusk was falling. We passed the pub, rectangles of light deep-set in its silhouette. It was the only two-storey building in the area, and it seemed that the entire community was parked outside it.

'Oh, there's Greg,' said Bridget's mother, quietly as if to herself.

Father Greg was walking out the door, his legs bowed by a wooden crate of beer, which he placed in the boot of his convertible. A surfboard poked up like a shark's fin from his passenger seat. He leapt over the closed driver's door, reversing with a screech.

We turned the corner and drove around the bay towards the lighthouse. We passed shabby beach houses, with their shorn or overgrown front lawns, their salt-cured fences. We drove down the gravel drive to the place where we would be staying. Girls' dorms to the right, boys' bunkroom off the common room. A patch of earth in the centre where we could burn off our frustration, a rotary clothesline to swing from at midnight.

Father Greg wasn't going to sleep on the premises. He was along the road with some old mates from varsity. He stopped by to bless the meal of sausages, peas and mashed potatoes, cooked by Bridget's mum. We bowed our heads and said amen.

Esperanza looked disgusted by her sausages and gave them to Bernadette, the captain of the Catholic girls' hockey team. Bridget molded her mash into a snowy peak. The boys turned sausage swallowing into a competitive sport. Kevin won: he ate eleven in eighteen bites.

After dinner we were miraculously unsupervised after Bridget's mum left with Father Greg.

'Get an early night, guys. Stick around here. Lotsa stuff to learn tomorrow. Yell out if there are any problems,' said Father Greg.

Kevin watched them through the window. 'They've gone,' he said.

'Cool. How about a walk to the lighthouse?' a boy suggested.

'Good idea,' said Bridget. 'I ate too much.' She prodded her concave tummy and made a fat-cheeks face.

'I think I'll stay here,' said Esperanza, her sketchbook opened on her ripped fishnet knees. I wanted to see what was in it, but Kevin was heading out the door. I pulled on my coat, and crossed the road to where the choppy sea pixilated the light from the ridge.

We made our way up the narrow path. Fences had been erected as gale breakers, but in the gaps the wind tried to push us off the cliff. The higher we climbed, the stronger the shove. I got vertigo, feeling the sea sucking me in.

'Long way, huh?' Kevin said. He had sought me out. He would soon reach for my hand. We would fall together or, if we were spared, kiss behind the lighthouse. 'Can I get past you?' he asked.

'Oh. Sure.'

He edged around me, then pretended to push me over the edge. I screamed, grabbing his arms.

'Not so hard,' he laughed, twisting out of my grip. Then he trotted ahead to repeat the trick on the other girls.

When we reached the top, I crouched at the base of the lighthouse. I followed the light around the bay, glancing off wavetops, illuminating Kevin. The boys jumped around the rocks, play-acting falling into the ocean. The girls interlinked their scarves and pressed their cheeks together. I wondered what Esperanza was drawing now.

Back at our quarters, a glass of water turned into a fight. Girls against boys. The water sprayed and arced; I slid across the floor. I staked out Kevin. As I came towards him he retreated to the boys' room. My hand followed, throwing the water through the door. He slammed it shut and the glass splintered. A piece cut deep into my thumb. I forced the door open and kicked. My foot landed somewhere soft.

'Bitch.'

In the kitchen I tried to staunch the blood. The boys had disappeared. I picked glass shards out of my palm. Esperanza helped me wrap my thumb in a teatowel. 'The intensity of this red is mind-blowing,' she said, as the blood soaked the checked cloth.

Jason, an emissary from the boys, appeared in the kitchen. 'You've destroyed Kevin's manhood,' he said. 'We'll have to get Father Greg.'

Esperanza dropped my thumb and followed the moans to the boys' dorm. I trailed petals of blood behind her but she shut the door in my face. Maybe it was the shock: I decided to follow Jason instead.

We weren't sure which house Father Greg was staying at, but only one was lit up. At the door there were crayfish pots and Red Band gumboots, a wind-chime made of driftwood, nails and pieces of sand-polished glass. We peered through the window at the tableau. A fire was going, and pieces of misshapen pottery hung on the wall. Father Greg's back was to us, but we could see him sitting next to Bridget's mum, a bottle of bourbon between them. Opposite sat a rough fisherman type pinching cards between his large red fingers. Next to him was a frizzy blonde woman, and a preppy man and woman sat at either end of the table.

The crayfish man opened the door.

'Can we talk to Father Greg?' asked one of the boys.

'Oh. Father Greg,' warbled the crayfish man from the doorway, mincing on his tiptoes. The frizzy blonde exploded in a fit of giggles. The preppy types smirked. Bridget's mum looked down, a smile on her lips.

Father Greg bristled. 'Now, what did I tell you jokers? Yes, Jason. What can I do you for?'

'It's Kevin. You gotta come and talk to him. He thinks he's infertile now.' Jason glared at me.

'He's what? You boys give him the snip or something?'

'I thought the Pope didn't agree with that kind of thing,' said the frizzy blonde, now breathless with laughter.

'No, Father Greg, *somebody* kicked him.' Jason shot another look at me, my thumb jammed in my armpit, which was now also stained with blood.

Father Greg sighed and got up. 'Can't leave you kids alone, can I? Now, don't you jokers nick my money while I'm gone. On second thoughts . . . ' He stuffed a wodge of cash into his jeans pocket.

'You can't bail now, not in the middle of the game!' roared the preppy man. 'What's become of you, Greg?'

'You tell me, mate,' said Father Greg.

'Yeah, I will tell you. You used to be a good honest fella. One of us.'

'Roger, watch it,' said the preppy woman.

'C'mon guys,' said Father Greg, yanking his coat off the hook, pushing us out the door.

'So where's Kevin?' he asked when we got back to the dormitory.

'In the bunkroom,' said Jason. The group clustered around Father Greg, but he went into the boys' dorm alone. The search-party boys paced outside the door like expectant fathers. Bernadette lined up the mugs for Milo.

After what seemed like an age Father Greg emerged. 'He'll be all right,' he said. 'But you should apologise, Katy.'

'But what about my thumb?' I asked. The bleeding had subsided, but when I unwrapped the teatowel, a chunk flapped and fresh blood welled.

Father Greg glanced over, turning pale. 'That looks nasty.'

The door to the bunkroom opened and Kevin swaggered out. The swelling must have doubled his balls in size.

'So, Katy?' said Father Greg.

I grimaced. The injustice of it all. Kevin looked angry but also triumphant. His eyes flicked the length of my body as though he were erasing me.

'Sorry,' I said, but not like I meant it.

The girls decided that the dorm room stank so they dragged their mattresses and sleeping bags to the communal area. I stayed in the dorm. Esperanza stayed too, sobbing into the foam mattress. I tried to comfort her, pushing a strand of her purple-black hair off her face, but she slapped my hand away and pulled her blanket over her head. I climbed back into my sleeping bag and gritted my teeth at the coiled springs of the bed above. I could hear shrieks and giggles coming from the lounge.

There was a man's voice, too; was it Kevin's? I hated him but I still wanted him to like me. My thumb throbbed beyond its circumference. I summoned a new Kevin scenario, a litmus test for my crush. We were on a boat in a calmer ocean. Each time the lighthouse beam passed me I had removed another item of clothing. But the fantasy Kevin wouldn't touch my nipple. He rocked the boat instead. The waves rushed over the side, claiming my clothes. He laughed at me. I dived over to retrieve my shirt, my pants, and then grabbed his arm to haul me back on board. But it came off. Its socket was pink, mushroom-shaped, like a doll's.

I was tired at the next morning's session. 'Ball-breaker,' Kevin hissed as we sat down with our photocopies and missals.

'Jack the Ripper,' I hissed back.

'Guys, gals, settle down. Let's bow our heads for silent prayer,' said Father Greg. I kept my eyes open. Father Greg looked wrecked, his skin puffy, his curls unravelled. Kevin jiggled as he prayed, face clenched shut. Bernadette's lips moved. Bridget looked hungry. Esperanza's eyes were open too, flashing when they met mine. 'Amen,' said Father Greg, and I bowed my head as if it had been there all along.

Father Greg outlined the morning's programme, chucking a hacky-sack into the circle of chairs. *Eucha-rist, recon-ciliation, forgive-ness, Love-thy-neighbour.* I missed it when it flew to me; it was heading towards my thumb.

'Try a bit harder, Katy,' said Kevin.

'Guys, guys, the world that God our Father and Jesus

Christ his son wanted for us was totally harmonious. Isn't that way-cool?' Father Greg said.

'No,' I said. The throb had moved to my head.

'What was that, Katy?'

'It was a bit sexist, don't you think?'

Everyone stared at me, adding to my adrenalin rush.

'Well . . . '

'Come on. Jesus surrounded by all these blokes — where were the women?'

'Jesus respected women. Look at Mary Magdalene. And he loved his mother, the Blessed Virgin Mary, deeply.'

'Then why can't women be priests, then? Why can't they use contraceptives? Why can't priests get married?' Two flags waved on my cheeks. Kevin stopped jiggling. No one squeaked their chair. Everyone watched Father Greg.

'Good question. Some of us think they should be able to. That might solve a few problems. But it outlines in the Bible that men should be the leaders. Women have a vital supporting role to play . . . '

Kevin laughed, then clapped his hand over his mouth.

'What, you mean they are the drudges?' I said.

'Do you call it drudgery reading the Word of the Lord to the congregation every week?'

'It's not as if they're the stars. They mainly do the cleaning, flower arranging and baking.'

'We have a gentleman in our parish who vacuums every week. It's not just the women who help out. Besides, it's a burden being a priest. Everyone wants something from you, but everyone has different needs.' Father Greg looked angry. 'How about we move on to reconciliation?'

'No! Let's keep on this topic!' said Jason, keen for a

fight. But Father Greg was already distributing the next set of photocopies.

Father Greg announced that the afternoon session would take place on the beach. Jesus was a fisherman among men, so it was fitting. 'Come on, boys,' he said, going into their dorm with a large plastic bag. They re-emerged in wetsuits, novelty T-shirts thrown over top. Father Greg was wearing a faded Virgin of Guadalupe, the back of it scrawled with signatures. 'See you down there,' he called out, jangling the keys to his convertible.

Father Greg wasn't using the prescribed session notes. He talked about Jesus walking on water instead, sneaking glances at the waves. After a while he called it quits, and everyone whooped. The boys leashed their boards to their ankles and jogged out to sea.

Bridget, Bernadette and the rest of the Catholic school girls opened their bags to reveal *Cosmopolitan* and *Who Weekly* magazines. They rolled up the sleeves of their T-shirts and hiked their skirts up to their knickers. Esperanza stood up and stretched. She dropped her bag beside me, not seeing the flap slide open, her sketchbook slip out. She wandered off along the beach, her black clothes flapping around her.

What was inside it? I imagined foetuses, skeleton Goth-princesses. I knew I shouldn't look. I should wait and ask her to show it to me.

But she was far away, and the other girls were shrieking over orgasm tips. My fingers crab-crawled sideways.

I was disappointed at first. The pictures were good, but were of ordinary things. A boot. A lampshade. An orchid. There were words in between, but I didn't read them, thinking it would be a greater violation. The next page was a hand and a foot. It was too bony and hairy to be Esperanza's. Then, a nude. Definitely a male, the hips tapered, the buttocks taut. Something about the thickness of the neck seemed familiar. I turned the page. A portrait of Kevin. Just head and shoulders. I snapped the book shut. I shoved it into Esperanza's bag. I lay on the sand and burned. Did that first encounter mean nothing? Was it idle curiosity that made him ask me what I was up to? Or was he the kind of guy who would cheat on his girlfriend? Worse still, maybe Esperanza had met him on that same afternoon, and she had agreed to hang out, while I had not.

'Hey.'

I opened my eyes. A black shape, I couldn't make out who because of the sun. I sat up, wiping my eyes.

'I liked what you said this morning.' Esperanza sat down beside me.

'Thanks,' I said. Why did she have to be the only one who mentioned it?

'There is so much bullshit at the church.'

'Yeah. It's a man's world.' My words were chunks of apple stuck in my throat. 'I don't even know why I'm getting confirmed. It's so fucked up.'

'Me neither, but my parents would kill me if I didn't. My dad has this lacy white confirmation dress he brought over when he escaped from Chile, and he thinks I'm going to dress up as a bride on the day.'

'You'd look like Frankenstein's fiancé.'

'Wouldn't that be cool? But he's not letting me do makeup. He's hiring a beautician for that.'

'That's a little over the top.'

'He's always going on about how drab New Zealand women are. My Goth look totally riles him. He's so traditional; he'd kill me if he found out I have a boyfriend.' She looked away. 'Or, should I say, *had*.'

'What happened?' I asked, a watery hope flooding me, despite Kevin's two-timing. 'What happened?'

'We broke up. He thinks we're too much like brother and sister.'

'You are? You don't seem alike at all.'

'That's not what he meant,' said Esperanza.

'Oh,' I said.

'God, love sucks,' Esperanza said.

'Yeah, it does,' I agreed. At least she could refuse sex before she was dumped. Nobody had ever asked me. I hadn't even been kissed. 'Can I see your sketchbook?'

'No, it's private.' Esperanza's face locked up too. 'Nothing personal; I don't show anybody. Hey, check that out.' She pointed at the sea.

There were the surfers, Kevin at the helm, poised on the curl of a wave. The ocean applauded as it crashed them against the shore. But where was Father Greg?

He emerged a little later, festooned with seaweed, his face red with frustration. He dragged his board through the sand, and then he towelled it down and chucked it into the back of his car. 'See you back at the camp, ladies,' he said. He pulled his T-shirt over his head and accelerated. The orgasm girls giggled as he fishtailed along the gravel road.

A month after camp I got confirmed. I almost pulled out, but I had transferred an Irish rock star into my fantasies, and didn't want to repeat the experience if I happened to marry him.

Esperanza sat between me and Kevin in the front pew, mortified in her blue eye-shadow and pink lipstick. The girls whispered loudly behind her, but Kevin hissed at them to grow up. It could have been my imagination, but I thought I saw his fingertips under her white lace thigh. It still felt like he was cheating on me.

Father Greg wasn't there to preside. The bishop would be anointing us, and old Cardinal Phillip had been shaken out of retirement to do the rest. His voice quavery, he informed us that Father Payne had departed on urgent missionary work, but wouldn't elaborate. The congregation snorted and shifted in their pews, exchanging loaded glances.

Bridget wasn't there, and the pew where her family sat was empty.

Ali and I had seen her the previous Friday night. She was smoking cigarettes with the boys who drove their Ford Escorts around the Square. I said hi, and she was about to ignore me, but then she spun round, her tartan mini-kilt flaring out. She was punkier than she had been at camp, an extra couple of studs piercing the cartilage of her ear.

'How's your mum?' I asked her, because I couldn't think of anything else to say.

She looked at me incredulously. 'You mean you haven't heard?'

'Heard what?' I asked.

'Huh. I was wondering why you came over. It's cos you're not part of the Catholic mafia. Maybe I should switch to the state school.'

'Tell me,' I said, a whinge in my voice. It seemed I didn't know anything about anyone.

Bridget threw her cigarette onto the footpath, crushing it beneath her steel-capped boot toe. She took a swig from a hip flask. 'You'll find out sooner or later.'

We lined up, and one by one knelt in front of the bishop. He painted crosses on our foreheads with oil, blessing us in his gentle voice.

I dipped my finger in the holy water as I left the church, using it to rub off the oil. I didn't want a cruciform of pimples. I walked down the steps into the too-bright sunshine and click of cameras, a freshly minted adult in the Catholic Church. I could make up my own mind now.

When she'd told him about Emmy, he had swung her in a circle and bought her a gelato.

That IMMORTAL SEA

Stella hadn't meant to get pregnant. The first time was an accident. But there they were again, two blue lines giving her the fingers. 'Oh no,' said Rick when she waggled the test in front of him. 'But Emmy's hard work enough — are you going to offload another one on me?'

She thought he would be happy. When she'd told him about Emmy, he had swung her in a circle and bought her a gelato. But that was three years ago in Paris, before the morning sickness started. Over another baguette dinner they had decided to go home and get real jobs. Stella's mother wired them the plane ticket money. Once back in their too-small flat they realised they had bypassed their career paths. Now, Rick was working nights in a bar, and Stella's days were spent eating fire or posing as a statue.

She'd got the idea when they'd lived in Barcelona. If only they were still there, drinking in Picasso's bar with the Lost Circus boys, dancing in clubs with outrageous names. Stella couldn't imagine a place called Your Cousin's Cunt here. She'd filled a stack of notebooks on Las Ramblas, sketching gypsies, Gaudí buildings and street performers. She was fascinated at how the statues could silence their bodies. She would drop a few pennies into their hats after she had sat there for half an hour, and even though they barely moved, they transmitted their disdain at her stinginess.

She'd spent days in a draught-free room with one of the Lost Circus boys, Jed. He'd taught her how to dampen her mouth with spittle and close off her windpipe. He'd shown her how to taste the flames, and how to hold them, still burning, in her mouth. Then how to suffocate them. He'd demonstrated how to blow dragon plumes of fire, but made her promise she wouldn't until she was very experienced. The blankets and fire extinguisher nodded in agreement.

Stella had taught herself how to be a statue in the first lonely months of Emmy's life. She knew about stage makeup from drama school; she had been to yoga and meditation classes. She tapped into her childhood love of Narnia, where Edmond discovered the hall of stone animals and mythical creatures. She practiced her micro-movements, aware of the powerful effect of a flared nostril in a frozen body.

On hot days Stella was a naked Greek goddess, her pale skin marbled, her pubic area obscured by a g-string-cum-grape-leaf. She could more or less apply the thick white body paint by herself, but she needed Rick to paint the grey fissures along her spine. She would recline on the side of a fountain, the boy who emptied his vase playing Eros to her Aphrodite. Her mother had warned her about cold concrete and piles, so she had fashioned a discreet flat rubber cushion to map the curves of her buttocks. But still she worried about blood clotting in her veins, her body freezing inside and out.

'Don't stress about it, Stel,' Rick said. 'Just think of those office stiffs. They sit at their desks all day — all they move are their fingers.' Luckily nobody stopped to watch for more than fifteen minutes, so she could do speedy asanas to remain supple.

On cooler days she was an angel. She could wear clothes here, sometimes sneaking a white merino singlet underneath her heavenly chiffon. This guise was taxing as well as warming. The wings were heavy, the white vinyl straps cutting into her shoulders, and she had to hold her arms up, as if waiting for a peach to drop from the heavens. She stood on the church steps, fretting about deep vein thombrosis, and whether or not she'd be let past the pearly gates in this outfit. As she stood she made up lots of poems, but they flitted from her head by the time she relaxed to write things in her notebook.

Stella imagined more sensible jobs for herself. As a child she had wanted to be a doctor, but that was before she auditioned to play Pinnochio. Maybe she could still be a library or gallery assistant. She would avoid the pigeon shit, the winds, the insults thrown at her reasonably attractive body. But the streets were so interesting. She saw men dressed in sheepskins and bells; she saw couples divorcing over bad restaurant choices. She saw babbling prophets and families of quadruplets, polka-dotted punks walking Dalmatians. She would miss all that behind a desk; she felt it was important research for her undisclosed future. Each afternoon she would gather up her hat full of coins and observances and return to Rick for a few hours before he started his job, telling herself that regular couples had no more together time than they did.

Rick didn't like the idea of Stella naked on the street any more than he liked fire-eating. 'But I'm not naked,' she would explain. 'I'm wearing body paint.' He had become more conservative since they had had Emmy. They had first encountered each other at drama school, where their starring roles required them to strip. Stella was alerted to their mutual attraction during the (un)dress rehearsal. The director had warned them about this, explaining that it was just a natural, physiological occurrence, accentuated by nerves, and they weren't to take it personally. Stella knew better. They resumed rehearsal halfway down the drive behind the camellia bush, ten minutes after the rest of the cast were dismissed.

That was seven years ago. Things have cooled since then. Stella was surprised that she got pregnant, given the infrequency of sex these days. It must have been the only weekend Rick had off last month. They didn't have a chance between their shifts. They focused on Emmy, and she lapped it up, giggling and flinging food, and making Mummy and Daddy read the same story over and over again.

'You're not going to continue being a statue, I hope,' Rick said after she had shown him the latest test result.

'Nice try, Rick.'

'No, I mean it. That paint smells like shit. I'm sure it's packed full of zinc. Don't you think it might poison the foetus?'

'So you'd prefer me to get elephant feet waitressing?'

'Well . . .'

'It's non-toxic face paint, Rick. And I don't want to go back to a café. The smell of tuna salad would make me gag.' As it was, she couldn't manage the pancakes and maple syrup Rick had made to celebrate her taking a day off work. He'd poured Emmy one in the shape of a dog, and she was pulling off its ears and shoving them into her mouth. 'More map-ul surp! More map-ul surp, peese!' she cried.

Stella hoped the nausea wouldn't last as long as it did last time. The hormones had made her want to puke day and night until she was eighteen weeks gone, and when they finally subsided she thought the baby had died. The midwife had to make a special call to reassure her that everything was all right.

Ever since she'd suspected she was pregnant for the second time, she could feel the baby moving. It was probably her hysterical alter-uterus, lodged in her brain. But she could sense a fizzing, a bud unfurling, beginning its circus swoops and dives. She had read that second pregnancies were easier because your body remembered what to do.

She had reconfigured her stomach with salutes to the sun, until Rick yelled at her to stop that goddamned hippy thumping. Maybe her muscles were too tight to accommodate a new baby. And what about the glasses of wine she had drunk with her dinner up until now? Would the baby have foetal alcohol syndrome, its eyes melting down its head like a novelty candle? She had been drunk when Emmy was conceived, and Emmy seemed fine. Pretty, even, with her copper ringlets and her pink cheeks. She hoped this baby would also be spared.

'Shall we do something? Go to the park?' Stella asked.

'Actually, I was hoping I could have a day to myself. Since I do most of the childcare. I was going to go around to Jeff's and have a band practice.'

'Oh. Okay.' Stella knew that under ordinary circumstances he would take Emmy along, and she would pluck away at Jeff's second guitar, pulling vital leads out of the amplifier. Was that childcare? Emmy would be deaf by the time she was three, but Rick said she was a rock'n'roll baby. She'd be signing a deal with Sony at sixteen. They could be showbiz parents and quit their shitty jobs forever.

Stella sat on the floor with a gluestick and a pile of dyed chicken feathers. She made tacky snail trails across a sheet of coloured paper. Emmy slapped on the feathers, and scribbled around them with her felt-tip pen. 'Dot, dot, dot!' she said, pushing the nib into its plastic barrel. 'I draw a giraffe.' Stella left Emmy to it, conscious of her own mother's need to control, and Stella's fear of making mistakes. Her mother believed that things were not worth doing unless they were done perfectly. She had kept Stella's neat drawings, throwing the unruly ones away. Stella had boxes of Emmy's efforts in her cupboards, taking up shelves that would soon be needed for baby clothes.

Why should Rick have the day to himself? She had stayed home from work so they could remember what it was like to be a couple, not to merely have a functional working relationship. She knew she had to give him a bit of freedom, that he had to recover the pieces of himself that were posted down the side of the sofa by Emmy. But she wouldn't be able to smile at him when he returned, strumming his crotch-level air guitar. She would let him dish his own dinner out of the congealing pots on the stove.

'Stop that, darling,' she sighed, realizing that Emmy was applying gluestick to the coffee table, slapping feathers there too. She'd salvaged the table from a skip. It had bow legs and blistered varnish. It looked better with Emmy's additions.

Rick didn't bother coming home that night. He called from Jeff's: he would head straight over to work. They were on to something, maybe had enough tracks for an album. 'Oh,' said Stella, hanging up the phone halfway through his 'Love you, doll'. Did he? Did he really? She had read in a magazine that men often loved their partners more once they'd seen them give birth. That wasn't the case for Rick. It was as if all the endearing bits of Stella had been transferred to Emmy, and once she had expelled the placenta, there was nothing left inside her to love.

Did she still love him? Today she wasn't sure. Their relationship was on hold, and the hold music was the Charlie Chaplin theme tune rendered on a Casiotone. Eventually, after Emmy went to school and the new baby was three or so, she hoped he would pick up the phone and they could carry on their conversation. But maybe they should just hang up now.

Emmy wasn't having any of her bean casserole. She was fishing out beans, squashing them between her fingertips, then hurling them across the room. 'Daddy! Where Daddy? I want Daddy!' she kept on yelling, pounding her fists on the table.

'Daddy will be home early tomorrow morning,' she explained. 'He'll kiss you goodnight at three.'

But Emmy didn't know when three was, so she kept on pounding, dislodging more of her casserole from her Bunnykins plate.

'Eat your dinner so you can see your bunnies,' Stella cajoled.

Emmy upturned the plate, then wiped the sauce away with her fingers. 'Bunnies!' she announced, showing Stella proudly.

'That's it, young lady, dinner's over.' Stella plucked her out of her chair, and Emmy imprinted tomato sauce on her green silk shirt — too good for around home, but she didn't see a dinner invitation coming soon. Stella ground her teeth. She could never be a solo mother. The stain was reason enough to try to make it work with Rick.

She went to bed a little after Emmy. They were both exhausted. Stella's body was whirring, multiplying cells, fashioning a placenta bead to string off an umbilical cord. She opened up her book, but within minutes it slipped out of her hand.

She slept fitfully. Her subconscious was aware that she had not had an adult conversation since breakfast. She dreamed of planes, she dreamed of the Lost Circus boys. She dreamed of her grandmother, who had been dead for three and a half years. Stella wished she had come home for the funeral. In her dream her grandmother sat with her back to the sea, her legs opened in a V. Her mother kneeled on one side of her opened legs, and Stella on the other. Around them washed the waves, foaming their skirts. They were digging a hole, stopping when her grandmother found something small to slip into her pocket. Stella cried pungent tears into the hole. She wondered where they came from.

Emmy woke her the next morning, calling for milk. Stella nudged Rick, but he grunted and buried his moss-breath in his pillow. Untangling herself from her sheets, she went next door to help Emmy out of her cot. Emmy's plump legs wrapped themselves around her waist, her arms around her neck, and Stella felt like a mother chimp, wading through the forest.

Her dream bubbled up as she stirred the porridge, as did lines from a half-forgotten poem. Emmy ate silky slices of peach from the can and the juice soaked her pyjamas.

Though inland far we be,
Our souls have sight of that immortal sea
Which brought us hither,
Can in a moment travel thither.

Wordsworth's notion that souls were washed in and out by the sea had stayed with her. Her grandmother appeared between the tides last night. Her doorstep had always been covered with seashells, driftwood, sand-blasted glass and pumice. Her handkerchiefs were kept in a camphor box. She was never without a jar of pepper-mints. Stella missed her. Why had she visited? Had the sea made a mistake in spitting out her soul? Or did her grandmother have a purpose?

'Mummy is a statue! Mummy is a statue!' Emmy announced, watching Stella apply her daily skin. Emmy poked her finger into the pot and blobbed it on her nose, giggling.

'Rick, can you get up? I need you.'

Rick groaned in the next room.

'Rick, I've got to go. Get the hell up.'

'Fuck, not this again,' she heard Rick say.

'What again?'

'This prickly pregnant bitch. I'm not sure that I can stand it.' Rick stood in the doorway in his boxer shorts, scratching the line of hair that descended from his navel.

'Well, once you marble me I'm out of here. Be grateful you don't have to swell.'

'You don't have to go through this, you know,' said Rick.

'Yes, I do,' said Stella. Funny that. She had gone on pro-choice marches. But the thought of having an abortion, well, she couldn't do it. 'How can you say that?'

'Have you seen our bank account lately?' said Rick, scrawling grey paint across her back. 'We may as well close it, it's such a joke.'

Stella threw her long-sleeved mumu over her head, wrapping her caked hair in a chiffon scarf. People looked at her strangely on the bus all the same — she didn't know why she saved her face and hands for town. At least this way she didn't imprint Emmy when she kissed her goodbye. She avoided Rick but he stood at the window with Emmy, blowing kisses that ricocheted off the glass and never quite reached her.

It was hot today, and she was melting. Not just her makeup, her resolve. She felt unwell. The pigeons cooed, dropping white shit on invisible typos. One landed on her arm, digging its sharp red claws into her. If it hadn't been for the $5 note someone was putting into her hat, she would have clouted it. This stillness was making her lightheaded; the fizzing in her womb was turning into an ache.

'Wow, that's worth some cash. That's grotesque.' A black-coated boy, his fingers encased in hinged silver rings, his face too thin and pimply, was peering at her. Grotesque? What did he mean? She had seen photos of herself in this guise, and even her mother acknowledged she looked beautiful.

'Yeah, man, that looks so real. Better than the stuff off the internet.' His friend was wearing a top hat and a cape. His eyes slid in two different directions beneath their white contact lenses.

What were they talking about?

Suddenly her womb clenched and she felt slick between her legs, beneath her hip.

'Fuck, man, it's real. Gross!' said the hinged-finger boy, dropping $10 in the hat, grabbing his friend by the elbow. They ran off, giggling.

Stella sat up. She looked down. There were clots of gelatinous blood on the concrete. She tried to stand but she couldn't.

'Oh my god, look at the fountain,' she heard a voice behind her say. She turned and stared at the water. The blood was swirling out in silky threads, clouding in the middle. As she watched, the cloud got bigger and redder until the blackness overrode it. Then the world was very distant and the water was soft and warm, and she wondered whether she was being born again.

Stella sat on the edge of a high bed, her body scraped clean of makeup, her back cold where the hospital nightgown gaped.

'Make sure you eat lots of red meat,' the blonde, ponytailed doctor advised, handing her a zip-locked bag of uterus scans. She must have been Stella's age; she hadn't bummed around in Europe beyond her career expiry date. Stella imagined her spacious, well-appointed house. She admired her crisp diamond ring. Every day she could perform medical miracles, and have her small audience clap and bow. Why had Stella chosen the stage?

'But I'm vegetarian,' said Stella.

'Well, you could eat leafy greens, but it would take too long. I'll prescribe you some iron tablets. This haemorrhaging will have depleted your supplies.'

Stella took the prescription. She saw Rick and Emmy hovering at the door, Rick carrying the bag of clothes she had requested. She gestured for him to come in.

'Sorry it took us so long, love,' he said, kissing Stella's forehead. 'We had to transfer buses: there's no direct route.'

The doctor fixed him in the eye. 'You're going to have to look after your wife for a few days. She's been through a bit of trauma.'

'Course I will, 'cept she's not my wife,' said Rick with a disarming smile.

'Look after your girlfriend then,' said the doctor. 'And I'm sorry, we need this bed, so I'm going to discharge you. Make sure you get a ride home.' She stepped back and then paused, extending a finger to touch a lock of Emmy's hair. Emmy recoiled. 'Oh,' said the doctor, colouring a little. 'Isn't she beautiful?'

'We think so,' said Rick.

The doctor pulled the curtain around the bed, and in the moment before they were enclosed, she looked wistful.

'You would have liked the ambulance, Emmy,' Stella told her, hugging her daughter to her chest, burying her nose in her hair.

'Nee-nah-nee-nah-nee-nah,' said Emmy.

'I'm sorry, Stel,' said Rick.

'So am I.' And she was: sorry that she would have to return to her old life, robbed of expectation. But she didn't want to think about it. Not yet.

'Maybe it's for the best. It wasn't a good time for us.'

'For the best? Me haemorrhaging in front of everyone? What do you mean?'

'You know what I mean. We really have to sort ourselves out.'

Stella looked down at her naked, mottled feet. She was still bleeding, and she felt gluggy. The doctor assured her the baby was gone: it was only the size of a raspberry, its fingers webbed. She felt too tired for big decisions or life-mending plans.

'I was thinking I'd like to go to jazz school next year,' said Rick.

'How are we going to afford that?' Stella asked.

'Maybe you could get a proper job.'

'I did well enough today. Check my hat.'

'Where is your hat? I can only see your mumu.'

'Shit.' They must have left it there when they loaded her up on the stretcher. Maybe somebody stole it when the crowd gathered around, fifty eyes glittering and retreating.

'I don't have enough to cover a taxi,' said Rick.

'I can't walk home. And look at Emmy.' She was lolling on the bed, playing with the folds in the starched pillow-case.

'Hold on a sec.' Rick left the room, and Stella played with Emmy's toes. 'This little piggy went to market . . . '

'No! Don't tickle me!' Emmy slapped her hand away.

'Listen, Emmy,' said Stella. And from down the corridor there were strains of a song — was it 'Moon River'?

'Daddy!' giggled Emmy, and she slid off the bed and ran down the hall.

'Here's our $20,' said Rick, returning with Emmy on his shoulders. 'They gave it to me to shut up.' He glanced sideways with a smile. 'Nah, actually that foxy doctor fronted up with it after I told her our situation. I'd like to think it was me, but she was more keen on Emmy.'

'Did you have to?' said Stella. She felt stripped of enough dignity as it was. She pulled on her shoes and her jeans. She zipped up the hoody that Rick had salvaged from the washing basket, daubed with Emmy's purple paint. At least she was dressed.

Stella sat in the taxi, head tilted back, watching the stars glide past. She thought of her dream. Her grandmother hadn't been washed ashore by accident. She had come to collect another soul. The tears were for two, and they had been cried in advance.

No wonder she felt so spent. Tomorrow she might sob into the porridge. She might cry at the daytime soaps. She might kick the door for her lost hat full of money. It *had* been a good day: she could picture at least $50, and she'd only made it to lunchtime. Tomorrow she might yell at the mother with the newborn who jumped the supermarket queue. Tonight she would be empty, her emotions absorbed by a maternity pad.

Rick reached over Emmy to squeeze her hand. 'I'm going to call in sick, love,' he said. 'I want to look after you.'

And his eyes sparkled, the sodium streetlights tinting his tears.

as a child
he dreamed
he was
pursued
by a wolf
with a tongue
like a piece
of luncheon
sausage

AXMINSTER

NOW, THE HOUSE

From the road, you can't see that the house is full of hay. You think the windows are reflecting the rippling grass. You follow the path up to the veranda. You take a big step over the broken step. You knock with the ring inside the lion's mouth, just in case, and when no one answers you turn the doorknob and pull it towards you.

The hay is as high as your forehead. You scramble up it, then you are in the hall. If you stand you can touch the ceiling, the mould making the plaster grapes look like varicose veins. If you crouch, you can run your fingers up the jasmine-patterned wallpaper until you reach the cornices. If you stretch your hand down into the hay, risking mouse bites and needle pricks, you can flick the heavy switches, but the lightshades will remain dark, the sockets blind, the glass petals furred with dust.

To the left of the hall there is the top half of a room. It is elegant in dimensions, a grand fireplace surround rising out of the hay. Through the wobbly, dirt-streaked bay windows there are roses. They straggle towards the sky, tall enough for Jack's giant. But this house should be Rumpelstiltskin's.

You make your way back to the hall. In places the hay is loosely packed, and you can slip under the surface. You wonder whether there are secret tunnels, caves of gnomes living at floor level. You tell yourself you are not afraid of spiders. There are more rooms, smaller ones, some with furniture poking up through the hay, carefully packed in case of breakages.

Each half window has a different panorama. From one you can see apple trees, from another pines. From the rooms on the other side of the hall you see blue hills against a pink sky. You don't make it into the kitchen. The hay has been stuffed to the ceiling, suffocating it. And then it seems as if it is stealing your air too, so you wade back as though your shoes are filled with wet sand, your breath skimming your lungs. You turn the handle of the door, which has somehow slammed shut, and you burst into twilight.

THEN, THE DREAM

Arlo doesn't often remember his dreams, but this one feels familiar. As a child he dreamed he was pursued by a wolf with a tongue like a piece of luncheon sausage, teeth like barbed wire. This time he is in that house. The bright living room where he and Mary drank a congratulatory sherry is obscured by shadow. There is a space behind the sofa for him to hide from the man who is walking down the hall, but if he hides then he can't shut the door. The man is strong; he will break the latch. What does he have in his hands? It is mercurial: a serpent, a gun, an axe, and even though Arlo is running across rooftops, trampling on cabbages, catching trains, the man is close, swooping, flying, breathing on his neck.

The light is grainy when he opens his eyes in his own home next door. Mary emerges like a silver gelatin print in its bath. She works so hard, he must leave her to sleep while the children do, but he is curdled with anxiety, he needs her to comfort him. He pulls a strand of hair off her cheek, straightens the blankets over her shoulder. He lies down and closes his eyes. But then the dream resurfaces — the man, the cabbages. It is as if he has stared at a lightbulb and its relief is burned on the back of his eyelids.

Mary, he says. He shakes her shoulder. She groans.

Iss-morning? she mumbles.

I had a dream. It seemed so real. Like someone was in the room with us.

Whad-happen? she asks, not really awake.

But he doesn't want to say, for fear that he will make it come true. If he swallows, his stomach acids could dissolve it. Nothing, he says. Go back to sleep.

He stares at the ceiling until the children open their doors and run down the hall.

NOW, THE NEW BLOKE

The horse's nose is like a peach, and that gives you the idea to feed him one. It is the end of summer, and you have stolen a golden queen from the case to be bottled. You take a bite: you want to make sure it is sweet. You place it in your flattened palm and offer it over the fence. The horse's nose quivers, then his lips flubber, soft and wet against your fingertips. You close your eyes because you do not want to see the blood if he misses. He munches on the orange flesh, the stone clunking against his teeth. He lets the peach fall, kicking it with his unshod foot. He returns to the grass.

Funny to see horses back in this paddock, Grandfather Arlo says. New bloke must have a way with them. Mine wouldn't graze there if you tied them to the fence.

Why not, Grandad?

They can smell what happened.

What? What happened here?

Never you mind. I shouldn't have said anything.

But Grandad, you can't say that. I need to know.

What you need is your dinner. Time to head back; Mary will be worried.

You glance at the house with its yellow hay eyes, its red-door mouth, its grey roof hair. Come and roll in my hallway, it winks. I'll tell you what happened.

No! you say. You realise you have spoken out loud.

Aren't you hungry, dear?

Of course, Grandad.

He shrugs, and you follow him along the gravel road.

THEN, THE END OF THE WORLD

Arlo was shifting the stock up the gravel road, get-in-behind-Tip, around-the-side-Wag. Feeyoooeeeee, went his whistle, and it glanced off all the dew on the grass, hit the hills and hurtled back at him. Baaaaa, went the sheep. Baaaaa. Each sound pinged in the blue stillness, and he was happy to be out there in his mended socks and his well-worn boots, his hound's-tooth cap on his head. He was happy to hurry the sheep with his stick and his dogs, his mind free for thoughts of Mary, persistent enough to drown the dream in his well of bad things.

It was Tim who broke the news, leaning over the gate, as if he had been waiting all this time. He only had the characters and the props, nothing more to make sense of it. So much blood. Didn't know who was going to clean it up. Seemed like the family was gone, although Colleen was still breathing when the ambulance came.

Arlo could hear the crank of bucket rising out of water. I don't understand, he said to Tim. Stuart seemed so, well, normal. He went to church, didn't he?

Yup, said Tim. Every Sunday. Used to bring the children by himself when they were young. Colleen wasn't the religious type. Had to convert to Catholicism when she married him, but it never really took. I dunno why. You can't tell about people. At least, that's what I'm coming to think.

NOW, THE CARAVAN

The caravan is fringed by the woods you are no longer allowed to play in. It is painted the colours of your teacher's parakeet: green, red, blue and yellow. Aluminium pots hang from hooks along the back door, and plants grow in windowboxes. They do not look like your grandmother's flowers or vegetables. Their leaves splay out in serrated stars. You saw the caravan being pulled along the road by an old Holden, and you thought the gypsies had come to stay. But there is just one gypsy, and Grandad says he owns the land now.

The Holden isn't there: the gypsy must have gone to town. You climb on the runnerboard and peer through a quarter window. At first you can't see anything, but then your eyes adjust. You make out the crumpled blankets on a bed. You see a small sink piled with dishes. On a table there is an enamel plate half filled with baked beans. When you hold aside the plants you see a workbench, scattered with miniature tools. There are small pliers, a hammer with a pea-sized head, a vice like a bulldog clip. Alongside the tools are chewing-gum lumps of gold. Some lumps have been rolled into worms, some smoothed into rings. You wonder how rich he must be to have all this, or whether, like Rumpelstiltskin, he transforms the hay from the house next door. The window is open a crack; you think about wriggling your fingers in to catch a gold worm. But then you hear the sound of tyres spitting gravel and you leap down and run, a leaf from his star plant still in your hand.

NOW, THE REQUEST

The new bloke has dropped by: Arlo has to empty the house out.

He has ignored that letter for too long. It came from Colleen's niece, postmarked a month or so ago. Colleen has gone to a rest-home now. Her desiccated brain rattles in its walnut shell and the relatives have power of attorney. They sold the house that Colleen refused to return to, but wouldn't do anything with. They didn't get much for it, given the state of the place, but enough to pay Colleen's fees for the next ten years, or however long it took. The niece thanked Arlo for keeping an eye on it for Colleen, but they both knew he hadn't done a good job.

What was he supposed to do? There had been no talk of renting, and the empty house invited back the children's ghosts. So he stuffed it full of hay. He packed it in so that nothing could rise up from the floorboards: no blood, no bones, no axes. No Stuart. Each year that he had a good harvest he would stuff it a little more, eliminating the spaces. He didn't mind about the nice pieces of furniture. Colleen had had her chance to move them up north with her. Mary certainly didn't want them in her house. So they will still be down there: the twin beds, the train sets, the bedside tables and lamps. Arlo will leave them to the new bloke; all he'll remove is the hay.

Funny sort, the new bloke. All those bits of metal stuck in his face. He reminds Arlo of the pig his mother kept. His father had taken Arlo out to witness its death, hooking his finger through the ring as he slit the pig's throat. Arlo transposed the pig's screams to those of Stuart's family, even though he hadn't heard a thing.

He wonders how the bloke keeps from going cross-eyed with that post pushed through the soft piece of skin above the bridge of his nose. He seemed friendly enough when he introduced himself. He was small. Not a dwarf, but not much over five foot either. A jeweller. Strange job for a man. He said he was going to set up his studio in the front room of the house, once he'd made a few repairs. Wanted to get on to it right away, if Arlo could do something about his hay.

Arlo had nodded. He'd shift it before the end of the week.

NOW, THE RING OF TREES

You are sitting on the stone steps, collecting fossilised snails' shells. You call them witches' pennies. You have found six already, you are looking for your seventh. When you have uncovered your last one you will be safe to walk down the path that leads into the woods. You will be invisible. You turn over a leaf and there it is. Or is it? The spiral that normally cuts through the middle is absent. It is also larger than the others, a scone in a plate of cinnamon pinwheels. You give it the benefit of doubt and you place it in your pocket. Your charm is complete.

There is a mosaic of light on the forest floor, dappling the fern fronds that brush your ankles. Your legs are bare, the scratches are light but they sting. You know that nettle is good to drink as a tea but you can't imagine how people can get it down their throats without them swelling up.

You see him in the clearing. He is standing there, his back to you. He is only a little bit taller than you. You think at first that he is a boy but then you see tufts of beard sprouting beyond his ears. You walk around the circle of trees, confident in your insubstantiality, but twigs crack beneath your feet.

He turns towards you, eyes wide. At first you don't see it because you are distracted by the barbells of gold that pierce his brow, his chin, his lips. But then you realise that he glints further down, and although you don't have brothers, you know what arcs from the V of his zip. He reddens, one hand covering his crotch, the other grabbing the axe that is wedged in the tree stump. You back away, you begin to run. You run out of the woods, down a different path, running, running until you come to the house. You clamber up the steps, open the door and force your way inside. This time, though, you don't alight on the hay. You dive into it, breast-stroking until you feel the floor beneath your hands. You are a needle. It will be impossible to find you here.

THEN, THE HOSPITAL

Mary has made Arlo come to the hospital with her, even though he said he had work to do. But Mary says it's important; they must show their support. She has left the children with her mother and now they stand at the foot of Colleen's bed, trying to see her through the forest of flowers.

I'm so sorry, Colleen, says Mary. She fusses with the roses from her garden, pushing them into the iron hedgehog at the bottom of the vase. If there's anything we can do . . .

Colleen doesn't respond. She turns her head to the window and stares. Arlo can see the finger and thumb bruises on her neck. It's only been a couple of weeks, but enough time for her family to be buried while she lay unconscious. They saved a space for her at the cemetery. Everyone's surprised she woke at all.

Mary plugs the silences. Such nice nurses, aren't you lucky. I remember coming here when I had Lucy and Michael. I stayed a week, but they were so bossy, I was glad to leave. You must have stayed here with your two. Oh, Colleen. How could–

Please, says Colleen. She closes her eyes.

I was only trying — says Mary. I only meant — ouch! She sucks the berry of blood off the tip of her finger. The offending rose keels.

Time to go, says Colleen.

Arlo and Mary back out of the room, relieved to be excused before the bad luck can settle on them. But before they can shut the door —

Wait. Can you look after my house? I won't be staying here.

Of course, Colleen, says Arlo.

She smiles only at him.

NOW, UNDERNEATH

Is this what it feels like to be buried alive? You remember the basket your Grandmother Mary gave you at Easter, all the little chocolate eggs hidden in the straw. You thought you had found all of them, but when your mother went on one of her cleaning jags, tipping it into the rubbish bin, another one fell out. You rescued it and ate it, even though the chocolate was rancid.

You wonder if other people have crawled in here and died. Are they matted in hay bandages like mummies? You learnt about sedimentary layers at school. Will they have turned into rock, a ribbon of red sandwiched between brown wood, grey carpet and yellow hay? You want to know what happened here, but you are scared that if you think too much about it, it might happen again.

It is difficult to breathe. The dark settles on your eyelids, forcing them shut. You remember Heidi's grandfather, who tucked a sheet around a mattress of hay for Heidi to sleep on. In the morning she ran across the mountain with Peter and the goats. But there is nothing to protect you from the prickly sticks, from its dust, its smell. You curl into a spiral, the shape of your witches' penny.

NOW, THE UNVEILING

Arlo backs his truck up to the veranda and climbs out. He unhooks the tarpaulin, pulling out a fork. He turns the doorknob, for the first time in years. It opens easily; he thinks the new bloke must have been exploring already. He takes a tentative forkful of hay, as if it were from a dish of foreign food. He unloads it on the truck. He is relieved to find that it is yellow, not at all stained. He takes another forkful, more bravely this time. He eats a hollow out of the doorway, crediting each bump and rustle to rodents. When he hits the ground he sees that the carpet is still there — thick with dust, but still patterned, a good-quality Axminster, not rotted or stained.

He is expecting to find bones, flesh, even though he was there for the funeral. He had watched as the coffins were lowered into the earth. He had thrown on a handful of dirt. But still, his nerves tell him otherwise, and when his fork comes in to contact with something soft and dense he screams.

The hay crests, arcs. Something is rising. He calls out. Who's down there? Who is it?

Sobs rising. Fingers emerging, grasping, flailing. Grandad, the voice says.

And he is gripping the warm hands, pulling, pulling.

The hay gives birth to his grand-daughter. Grandad, she sobs. There was a man. He had an axe.

I know, I know, he says. He strokes her golden hair. It's over now.

Several of these stories have been previously published:

'Notes on Etiquette', *Sport* 35, VUP 2007
'The Wrong Shoe', *Sunday Star-Times*, November 2006
'Just Married', dramatised for National Radio, 2005
'Stepping on Cracks', *New Zealand Listener*, Vol 195 No 3356, September 4–10, 2004
'Pod', *Creative Juices*, ed. Emma Neale, Harper Collins Publishers, Auckland, 2002